The Importance of Having a Rose

Amina Shalash

The Importance of Having a Rose

New Year's Eve, a rose, two worlds, and the soul in between

NB: the novel was previously edited by Linda Cleary
www.freewriterscentre.org

For Reem, Riad, Ziza and Bahey

Always be with me
Always share with me
Every moment that I live

ACKNOWLEDGEMENTS

I had just turned thirteen when I decided that I wanted to write a book. This dream seemed very hard to reach. I had to find inspiration everywhere and I had to be very patient.

I was sure that I wanted to be read, but at that time, I didn't know exactly what to write and HOW to write it.

I was always told that the beginning is the hardest part. I was trying to put into words the different ideas that I had in mind but the story of Rose has, a few years later, unexpectedly invited me to write it all at once without feeling it, and to leave behind any other story that I'd been trying to bring to life through words.

My writing journey is by far the best I have had (until now). It is an experience that has made me grow, and that has taught me a lot. Today as I am witnessing a dream come true for the first time, I am able to understand the importance of dreams. I hope that everyone who reads my book dreams more, and works very hard to make their dreams come true.

The story of Rose would have never been as it is without the presence of some people in my circle. I would love to acknowledge all the support and encouragement that has been given to me during my writing journey:

My mother, you promised me that I'll be a great writer long before reading my book. You are the only person in the world who never stops believing in me. Thank you for the trust and thank you for always being proud of me. I can never thank you enough for all the support you give me, the art, the love and the moments we share.

My father, when I first told you that I started writing a book I was thirteen and I wasn't sure if it was ever going to be real. You told me that you'll read it and that you'll publish it for me if you like it. Seven years later and we're here! Thank you for this shared journey.

Ziza and Bahey, I can never thank you enough for every moment we spend together. Thank you, thank you, thank you, for the laughter, the memories and the courage that you always give me (and for always being so excited to read this book although you never stop making fun of me).

Mamina, thank you for showing me the importance of being passionate. Having you in my life makes everything better. I hope I made you proud.

Shaimaa Alaa, this book wouldn't have been possible without you. Thank you for always telling me that I'm 'almost there'.

Dr. Tarek Okasha, thank you for helping me understand Rose more, and for taking the time to explain to me what she had.

Dr. Mohamed Fekry, you teach me patience and compassion and help me understand people, and myself. Thank you for being my anchor.

Madame Isabelle, thank you for the love of literature that you have always shared with me. Having you reading my essays out loud in class has surely motivated me a lot. My work is also very organized because of you. I was very happy to be your student, and very lucky too.

My family, you are the most precious gift I have ever received.

My best friends, you've been with me through every step of the way...Thank you for everything, especially the fun!

PREFACE

As I lived, I understood that not all beautiful stories are about love and that not all people who struggle, struggle from an illness. It was a surprise for me to slowly discover through Rose that a weakness can easily be turned into a strength and a source of happiness into one of unhappiness.

Half of the stories that we live, and live with, revolve around the way we feel, and the way a certain thing or person makes us feel. Half of the people that I know find their happiness in the happiness of the ones they love the most, and half of the people who were blindsided by something, live with the shadow of it inside of them forever.

Rose was a bit different, she was always torn between her weakness and her strength, lost between where life had put her and where she'd want to put herself.

Life is always like this, and we are like this. Full of weaknesses and of strengths until we let one win over the other and then it wins over us.

I wrote this story because Rose lies inside each and every one of us, not for her story with cancer or with love but for the way she admitted everything she felt, for the way she was never afraid of her weakness. Rose understood that hiding a weakness was already another weakness, that it's never right to run away from the way we feel, and how things are to us. It was a surprise for me to understand the way in which Rose had twisted life. Rose is sensitive and it's why sometimes she felt everything, and sometimes nothing at all.

Rose taught us that the strongest people are the ones who live every moment. Unafraid to get hurt. I came to the conclusion that strength and courage aren't the same thing... We are strong when we let things happen to us, when we accept change, take risks and open doors by ourselves.

As you read this story you will find out the truth behind Rose's cancer; it's far from what you thought it would be. Sometimes we create stories for ourselves and live with them. Sometimes we create pain and struggles out of nothing at all and start living every remorse of it. Sometimes nostalgia isn't enough to make us cry, so we look for a way to bring those tears out. Sometimes life happens to us in a very simple way, and some of us prefer feeling strong by finding a way through every complication than never being judged for their capabilities and strength.

Sometimes we think that happiness isn't a way of satisfaction, so we do more harm to ourselves than the world could ever do to us.

The Importance of Having a Rose does not only speak to our souls but also reveals the idea of hiding different lives behind our soul.

We are easily manipulated by everything we live with, and all that we are surrounded by, thinking that we are the ones who manipulate everything all the time. We fail to understand that if there's one thing that the universe has under control, it's without a single doubt the human beings that we are.

Don't try to understand Rose... The story is blurred in a way. You get lost every time Rose gets lost in her thoughts, and you find yourself as she does. She repeats herself sometimes. Rose is beautiful, I believe. We are all attached to the weaknesses, strengths, happy and sad moments we have.

The importance of having a Rose is somehow an approach of reality, a picture of every distorted mind struggling to put together the pieces of the puzzle that form the pictures in the memory. Detach yourself from Rose's story, then come back to it again. Do everything that you have never done with a book before. Feel free to write a note to Rose, or to a friend when you find a blank page at the end of some chapters, draw something if it's going to make you a bit happier. Write a big 'No' somewhere on your pages when you think that Rose does life the wrong way, collect a rose or two from a garden, or ask a florist to give you one, and slide it into the pages that tell the words that you like.

When you leave a book after finishing a story, it shouldn't be as clean or neat as you had it at first. I have always believed that the books that have marks of hands on them are much more precious than the books that are always crisp and well kept on shelves.

I'll see you soon.

ONE

Thank you to every cancer fighter, to every cancer survivor, and to everyone that couldn't come out of the war to the life they were in before, thank you for being strong enough to handle life alone. Thank you to every mother, every father, every grandmother, grandfather, aunt, uncle, sister, and brother. Thank you to every friend, to every stranger who never stopped loving life even after it tried to bring them down, or kill their minds.

Thank you to every lover, who was here to help their other half heal. Thank you to every person who managed to live with the stress that comes with every therapy.

Thank you to those who taught us how to stop saying sorry when we want to say thank you, to those who never left our side, and always managed to make our smile so bright.

Thank you to those who gave us enough love, hope and strength that we were able to give it all to other people too.

We are forever thankful for having you in our lives.

Thank you to that friend who inked my name on their wrist, supporting the war I'm in…

Thank you to the strangers who helped me hide my fears, to the ones who never knew my story but helped me shed my tears. Thank you to every person who has joined my campaigns, to every person who has walked for my sake. Thank you to life, for keeping me going with every little cell that remained in me. Thank you to my friends for growing a limitless feeling of constant joy inside of me.

Thank you to my sister, and the sister of every fighter, for donating her hair to me when she was only three. Thank you to my brother for holding my hand when I was shaking from fear. Thank you to my dad for being my hero and teaching me how to become a hero of my own. Thank you to my mother, for handling my case, for accepting to live in constant stress with me when she could have left me to sleep alone in every hospital that received me.

Thank you to every nurse that has held my hand as I walked through the corridors of the hospital, thank you to every doctor that has taken care of my body, thank you to every therapist that has taken care of my soul.

Thank you to my lover, for keeping my secret when I was afraid to let people know, for giving me the chance to heal alone, and grow stronger once more.

Thank you for leaving me so strong.

And finally, thank you to myself, for going through hell like I was going through heaven. Rose, if cancer didn't break you I don't think that anything in this world will be strong enough to do so. There's nothing else I feel like I want to say. I love my life the way it is and if I had the chance to change anything about it, I would not.

The importance of having me.

The importance of having a Rose.

The importance of having a little bit of me in your life. A light bulb to every darkness. You may never fully understand how it is, to not know yourself well enough. No one will ever understand how much I believed in the stories that my mind used to create. When you're unaware of the reality you're in, when you're nearly living another life, it's very hard to know whether the reality is a dream or the dream is a reality. It gets harder with time, and you integrate yourself more in your own fabrication of a life, because the mind knows what the soul needs, so it builds up for it in every dream.

From Rose, we will meet often.

TWO

A thousand ways to leave this place, but another ten thousand that will lead me back to it.

As a Rose, I need change. Constant change will always be my only remedy. But someone once told me that things can change to the point that they remain unchanged. Some people keep changing their minds so many times until they get back to that starting point.

Some moments are so different yet so similar, so are some people.

PART ONE: PRE-PARTY

'For someone I loved a long time ago,
For something I had a long time ago,
Here's to the pieces of my heart I left behind every time I
had to let you go.'
Rose

THREE

The party is loud. The music is blaring everywhere but in my room. I wake up. I'm lost. I don't know if it's day or night.

"Good morning," I shout from my room. Nobody answers, so I take a little walk in the apartment. "Good morning!" I repeat a bit louder. Nobody responds for the second time. I run to my sister's room, open her door suddenly and sit on her bed without saying a word.

"Good morning Rose," she says happily.

"Don't even try to talk to me," I say inside my mind.

Today wasn't my day. I don't remember any day being 'my day'. Things just happen to me. I tend to go with the flow, I tend to let things go with my flow. The music is always very loud in my sister's room. I never understood her. I fear crowds. I hate when people talk loudly. I hate words. I hate a lot of things that I never knew could be hated. My sister turned her speakers off in the middle of a song that I was enjoying. It was somehow waking up the ghost of me. I went to her. I slapped her on the face. I went back to my room. I cried.

The party is in a few hours. I'm not going anywhere. I party alone, in my room, or in my hospital room, if I'm over there. The 31st of this month is meaningful to everyone, except for me. I don't believe in new years. Life is made of one flow, we can't count the days, or cut our living into years. I'm crying. My curly hair is all over the place. My eyes are red. I went to the bathroom. I put my head in the toilet. I touched the water. I cried. I need to be good before tonight. I will talk to the people I like. I feel unloved. I feel the silence even when the music is loud.

It's a new year! It's going to be good, way better than any other year we have lived before. The music is loud outside, but here, in my room, the loneliness is unbearable. A feeling no word will ever describe. It's a long story to tell, always better when it's only felt. I need to walk on my own for a while, to trigger every emotion inside of me. I need to walk alone, to feel the wind inside of me. I need to cry and shout without having anyone wiping away my tears, because this one person who is always standing near is the one person who makes it all stop from being at ease.

You remember your loneliness, you start looking for your ghosts.

"They know that I love them anyway," I told myself as I started walking slowly. "They know the place they have in my heart. I once told them how special they are, how precious they'll always be to me, they must know by now that they're a piece of me."

I forgot how much I hated empty words, but every word of mine at that time was emptier than the one I spoke before it. We need to stop relying on the idea of 'love', because love is not the sweet dreams and the perfect images we have of things. Love is not this abstraction we all live with. Love is effort. Your family will only feel like your family when you stop thinking that they will love you no matter what happens, and no matter what you do. You have to understand that people walk away for a reason, or maybe because they couldn't find a good reason to stay.

"Life has reasons," the ghost inside of me said.

Love has its own reasons. Your best friend might run away. You might start hating your boyfriend because he doesn't kiss you as often as he did before, or simply because he is as absent as present.

"Love is time," my ghosts have always told me.

We will save the world when we start saving ourselves from these types of thoughts. Thoughts are toxic sometimes. We will go, and come back. We will try to change the world, until we realize that the world is also trying to change us. No, we won't let it win. We will do every possible act to prove ourselves stronger than everything that has created us. A voice will start whispering to us that the world is secretly trying to destroy us, that our death will prove this lie. We try to destroy the world before it destroys us. To bring Hell to Earth before Earth takes us to this 'other world'.

We start remembering how small we are. We find more reasons for us to unite and walk as one. You finally wake up. You start strengthening your circle of loved ones. You run back to those who will supposedly never stop loving you no matter how unloving you have become. You shout your first "I love you". You prove your first "I care about you".

You start bursting into tears every now and then when you remember that the universe will sooner or later take one of them away from you. They're going to the other life anyway, should this make you want to leave or care more and stay?

You close your eyes, get drunk for once, and at that time of the night you understand that you have to do it right. You will forget that they will love you no matter what by loving them more, and proving this idea right, every other night.

You want to be the one who loves more, because they'll be the same, they'll do the same, and this reciprocity only brings joy. You want to be the one who loves more, because your love is the only thing you can offer at the moment. I'm strange. You are stranger. You are a stranger. You judge people, but you are like them.

I'm far away. You probably never heard a word about me. But you will keep searching for me, until you find me, or until I find you, hiding somewhere in the universe. Or waiting for the universe to hide you.

You will get to know me, soon.

FOUR

Yesterday's dream woke me up in the middle of my sleep. A voice inside me whispered my name until the voice of my ghost screamed.

My mind was distorted. The Rose inside of me was starting to fade away. The ghost of me is taking its place. My life is a dream. Every dream of mine is a reality. Unlike anyone else in this universe, I'm only aware of who I am while I'm deeply asleep.

Yesterday, or last night to be more precise, as I was closing my eyes and imagining that I was closing the door of my mind, a thought knocked loudly only to start explaining to me the way that I was. I was navigating slowly in my own mind, walking in circles in a place where gravity is nothing but an illusion. We live in a world of illusions. I was naked. A flying hand covered me in a white ghost-like textile. Another lighted flying arm linked mine and led me to a therapist's chair. The place was unknown, undefined I must say. The place was impossible to determine because it was empty, abstract in a certain way. A voice from inside of me started explaining to me who I really was.

"Rose, you're good. You're going to be better." The voice disappeared. The voice faded away as it said those words. I tried to wake myself up from this weird and unexplainable dream, but I wasn't powerful enough to do so. I was in a very rare state of not knowing whether I was dreaming or lost in reality. It doesn't matter anyway. Both, my dreams and reality merge into one on some days.

FIVE

The Rose inside of me knows better; stories I never heard and moments I never lived. The Rose inside of me knows people that my eyes have never seen and feels people so easily. The Rose inside of me feels better, things that never stroke me no matter how intense they could feel. The Rose inside of me has always lived with me. In fact, my name is Rose. My name is real, so real in the way it reflects everything I am or will ever be. My parents named me Rose to reflect the beauty of a flower and the power of its fragrance. To bring the joy a rose brings and the feeling of love it creates. My name is Rose to remind the world that I am fragile, to remind the world that I need love and care. My name is Rose because I am precious to myself and to others, because I make others feel special. I cut myself into pieces to keep others whole, I make my scars dig deeper to heal the scars of all. I'm a Rose,

I'm as lively yet as lifeless as a rose could be, as mortal yet immortal as a flower could be.

I'm a rose because I have phases. I feel better so easily yet worse when the water is no longer free. I'm a rose because I shut down once every therapy, I shut down even when I'm cancer-free. My name is Rose. I'm a rose because everything that I do, roses do, and everything that I am, roses are. My name is Rose. I'm small, I grow. The beauty in me fades with time, the flower in me disappears in life.

My name is Rose and my story is real, my story is so real that I cry every time I remember how long it took me to heal. I'm fighting with myself. I'm in a war that no warrior has ever seen. I'm in a war and it's slowly killing me. I'm two steps away from winning but always a step closer to dying. I'm two steps away from losing hope but always one closer to gaining faith. I'm twenty-two, and my body has been eating itself up since I was seven. I'm twenty-two and I'm not any different from you or your friends, I'm just hoping my life does not end.

I've been here since I knew that my forever was about to end, since I knew that I would be gone soon, that I would lose my hair, my confidence and all that makes me feel good about myself. I'm twenty-two and I'm fighting a battle you will never understand but I'm enjoying every moment of my life like never before.

Yesterday I went back to my hospital room and I felt so down. I wish the doctors would let me go home. I miss my bed, I miss Mom's food, I miss the feeling of home that no other place has ever given me. I miss knowing how to cry and breaking down when I need to without being interrupted by a nurse comforting me every time. I miss too many things that can't really be described. I'm not any better here, I'm not feeling better, I'm not getting any better, my cancer is not healing. I have become weak. I can't feel myself, I can't even understand myself. I'm in a constant relationship with grief. I feel like death is coming soon.

The bone cancer hit me when I was seven. I fell on the ground after my ballet performance and it wasn't like any time I'd fallen before. It hurt so much. I was out of breath. I was crying and the pain was intolerable. My best friend held my hand but pulling me up was never harder, because of how much I was falling to pieces, even though I was so tiny compared to any seven year old girl anyone knows. She took me to the doctor's office who didn't know what to do with me, crying and screaming in such a way that the pain came out of my eyes. I couldn't talk, not even to describe my pain. Not a single red or inflamed spot was visible on my whole body. The doctor was confused. He wanted nothing to do with such a spoiled girl who excelled at acting, or at least that's what he thought. So he sent me back to my teacher saying that I was just finding a way out of the performance.

I had to go back on stage. I had to make every move perfectly. I had to perform a four minute dance with the posture of a ballerina and not forget to smile. My tears wouldn't stop from falling, and I fainted. It was no joke. The music stopped. The lights went out. The stage turned black. The audience couldn't understand nor guess what was happening on the other side of the room. It was out of the doctor's hands. They called the ambulance and my father. It was the very first time I had seen my father run like this. He was running to me in such a way that made me forget about my pain. He came to me. I opened my eyes to his kiss. I opened my eyes hearing his voice whispering, "You'll be fine." I wanted to hug him back but it was just at this moment that I discovered how much my bones really hurt. My hands were never like this, I was never like this. This time I had a bad feeling about it. I felt like something was going to happen to me and that it wasn't just hurting because of the fall. I imagined myself losing an arm or a leg. I pictured myself in a wheelchair, bed-bound, and if I had worse situations in my mind, I would have pictured myself in those also but being only seven I, thankfully, ran out of ideas.

A few minutes after this the ambulance came. Four tall men came down with some kind of black bed that looked so uncomfortable, that I wasn't even sure if it was a bed or a tray; a human tray, maybe. The last thing on my mind was the idea that I'd be the one carried on this 'tray', but it happened. They held me carefully just the way a curator might hold a piece of art. I felt fragile. It was at that time that I understood how fragile and sensitive I was.

They got me, carefully, inside the ambulance. My dad came in with me and held my hand the whole way. I couldn't explain to myself what was happening; I felt like a toy being transported from one place to another. It was a feeling I had never experienced before just like the feeling of torturous pain that had been with me for more than an hour.

I arrived at the hospital and by the time I was in my room, I had already broken down and cried a multitude of times. My eyes wouldn't stop delivering bitter tears. The pain was expanding all over my body. I wanted my doll. I wanted my games, my Disney themed room, and my favorite Winnie The Pooh yellow pajamas. I couldn't express my objection. I was a rebellious child at heart but weakness had shut this down.

Everybody left my room. I was alone. I felt so lonely at that time. The bed was huge. It had so many buttons on its side that I couldn't reach. This place wasn't designed for people my age. My legs couldn't even reach the end of the bed. The clock wouldn't move, not even a little bit. I was staring at the wall in front of me. I was thinking about all the fun I was missing at school. I started understanding at this moment that time is only a determination we have set to durations. It's abstract. It's unreal. Time is an illusion. The real time is felt and not lived. Everyone was having fun, except for me; playing hide and seek, and listening to Mrs. Diana's stories in the story corner without me. The story corner was my favorite place in the classroom; a place that was so empty yet so full of happiness. Mrs. Diana made this corner before the school year started, she had got us a nice carpet her grandma had once made for her and put some shelves where she placed books and cushions so we could relax while imagining whatever she told us in her stories.

In my hospital room, I was missing Mrs. Diana, and even more the feeling of being her favorite girl in class. I was missing every comment I gave that made the whole class make a lot of noise, and at the end, I was the only innocent one. I was missing everything already, everything related to every day, everything I usually did. But how could it be so fast, I had only been there for a few hours.

As a little girl who was always curious, I tried understanding why I was being held here for that long. It was unfair, I wanted to play dress up with Naomi because she always lets me pick the outfits I like. Naomi was my friend from art class, she was too beautiful to be real. Even though she was seven like me she was mature to the point that she didn't really care about me fighting for dress-up or that I wanted to do a certain thing. She believed that she'd enjoy anything, so she always let me choose.

My day had been gone for long, and I didn't want to sleep here. I wanted to sleep next to my mom. I cried. I cried so hard that it hurt me more. I hated being here. I hated being alone especially in a place like that one. It felt like jail, even worse. I felt like my dolls, when they were put back in the big pink box and left in the corner of my room for months. I felt isolated from reality. I felt like I was in another world, alone, with no one but my ghosts.

My imagination brought me everything that could have happened to me but I couldn't even begin to guess it right. I gave up on anything and everything for that night, I even gave up on being relieved from the pain. I was so still. The only moving thing were my tears. I closed my eyes, let my chin down so that it touched my chest, wrapped my arms around my body and slept. It wasn't a peaceful sleep, it wasn't anything that could even be compared to sleep. It was an escape. I dreamed of a plain black empty place, of death, maybe.

It was at four in the afternoon. I woke up the next day at eleven in the morning. I woke up to my mom, she was holding my hand and I opened my eyes as she slowly kissed my forehead. I almost felt the kiss in my hair. I smiled, but by the time I had opened my eyes, I was already crying, it was stronger than me.

"I want to leave."
"You are, very soon, Rose. We're going somewhere soon, don't worry."

The silence was killing me. Loneliness. Yes, now I understand what it is. My mom got me sweets and all kinds of goodies that I love. She told me that we were going somewhere together. I was overjoyed, but I didn't know that we were going somewhere inside the hospital. She held my hand and helped me get in the ugly wheelchair the hospital had given me. It wasn't pink, it didn't have princesses on it, not even flowers. It was black, it was made of the color of hell just like everything else in that place. I needed to leave. I vowed to cry every day until heaven found me, or until life found me a way out of here.

My mom tried to make it fun, she told me to close my eyes so I could enjoy the crazy ride she was about to offer me. She forgot that the wheelchair had four wheels, because she only used two, and she took me all the way through the hospital corridors as if we were spending the most memorable day in the happiest theme park ever. She got me to the left, then to the right, up then down.

"Are your eyes still closed? Oops, we're about to bump into the wall!" and many things like that. With a five minute ride she made me forget about my pain, about the place and most importantly about all that I was thinking of earlier. A moment like that made me understand why mothers happen to exist.

We arrived in a place that I could never have imagined. She said that we had to wait for our turn. There was a huge tube that got us somewhere like another room, and I was told that

44

I'd be put in this thing. I started crying telling my mom that the sound of this place was so scary, that I didn't want to be there, especially alone. I laid down on something that was so hard and the tube slowly absorbed me. I heard people talking about me getting an MRI, but I had no clue about what it was.

As the tube got me back out again I saw my mom crying like never before. My dad was sitting alone in a corner on one of those waiting chairs. He was different, his eyes were glowing. How could my dad get watery eyes for no apparent reason? I didn't do anything wrong. I was inside, I was alone, I forced myself not be scared of the sound of this place. I did so many things to show them that I'm strong like them, and at the end, they are the ones who became like me. I cried because they were acting strangely, they weren't even answering me. I cried because when I asked them what was happening to me, they burst into tears without saying a single word. I'm smart enough to understand that something serious just happened to me. I was smart enough to know the meaning of both my parents crying so painfully. I understood that they had also received the results of my blood tests and biopsy. I was done with everything already. I didn't want to go to school anymore. I hated everything especially the hospital. I cried yet again and a nurse came and took me back to my room. Before I got there, I had already hated her for everything she was and everything she did. I started hating everyone in that place, everyone in white, in black or in scrubs. I hated these two colors for whatever they represented in this place. I already saw black inside of me most of the time. All I could think was, "I have pain inside of me, I'm not the same anymore. I will never be the same again."

A few hours later, my mom and dad came in and kissed me as I was in bed. Shortly after that, they each pulled a chair up to the side of my bed and held my hand. They started explaining what had happened to me. They told me things I could have never guessed alone, things I never imagined that existed. They told me that my body had started eating itself up, and that's why my legs hurt the most. They then explained to me that my bones were eating themselves because I had too many cells and that what I had was called cancer. The only picture I had of this thing in my mind was the picture of weak people, losing their hair, and becoming more and more depressed everyday. I believed I would die soon, I heard the doctor talking about it to the nurses, and I then heard the nurses saying it back to my parents. I heard it twice, my ears did not lie to me. In my mind, I couldn't accept the fact that it was happening to me. It would have been less shocking if it were one of my friends.

That's selfish, but we all are. We all think that we aren't, but deep down, we love ourselves a bit more than we love anyone else. We want things for ourselves that we wouldn't want for anyone else. We secretly pray that the bad things happen to others, but never to us, if they have to happen. In a world of Roses, only the good exists… and a rose would only want all the goodness in the world for another Rose. Yes, we are selfish. Don't try to convince anyone that you are as caring about people as you are about yourself. Don't lie to yourself, we all lie to ourselves. It's too hard for us to accept some facts in life, but it's always harder if we hide half the world from our sight. We are weak enough to believe the lies we tell ourselves, we are weak enough to run away from every truth that hits us. We are always searching for a way to stay whole, we don't like surprises, we don't like change. We want something that will finish the straight line we started drawing when we were three, four, and five. But now that we are becoming older, it's very hard for us to understand that our hands don't have this ability, and nor do we, as we live our lives. We are not capable to walk in a straight line forever. We have to stop trying. We have to stop looking for that straight line in every city we move to, and every place we try to settle down in. It's alright to walk in circles for a while, it's alright to bump your head, to fall down. Appreciate the labyrinths you encounter, appreciate everything you don't understand, appreciate the difference, the similarities, the difficulties, the madness, the sadness, the illness, and everything that comes in your way. Appreciate the fact that sometimes you only understand something long after it's over, understand that life isn't about the moment, but about the memory the moment leaves behind, appreciate the fact that you might disagree with everyone. You might even disagree with yourself, with life, as a whole.

"Rose," said Tia, the head nurse of the hospital from behind my door.

I don't know much about Tia. The ghost from inside of me is also called Tia. I never know if it's the nurse who is talking to me or my ghost. I don't know. I don't know much about the ghosts I live with. I just know that they're here, all the time, and they talk a lot. They tell me a lot about the world we live in, and the world they come from. They take me for visits sometimes, I'm not sure if I like coming back from there.

A few minutes after meeting Tia, I decided to have a walk in the hospital. I was the youngest person there. I thank God everyday that no one younger than me at that time spent so much time there. I usually have long walks, I think alone. I love to spend time alone. I think of life as a dream, I think about everything that I want, and that is not here. I try to appreciate the things I have always hated or ignored.

I try to find reasons for the way I am and the way things around me are. I'm trying to understand why I hate some things so much, I'm trying to find a reason that I dislike the amount of people I actually dislike. I never really found any answer other than the fact that I hate everything that I don't understand, and hate everyone who doesn't make me feel as special as I really think I am, or as comfortable as I want to feel. It took me time to reach this point with my mind.

That day I walked for nearly an hour. I'm a wanderer, it's something that everyone who knows me, knows about me. I like taking myself to places, I get bored easily and I like to move a lot yet it's confusing because I'm afraid of change, I'm afraid of everything that isn't familiar to me.

I have cancer. I have lived all my life with cancer trying to fall in love more and more with my living.

SIX

I have to keep walking, to any place I am able to on my own. I have to keep walking, running if I can, because if I stop, my life might stop again. I hate the awareness that all I had might come back to me once more. I'm weak, even if I never show it to the world. I'm weaker than I've ever known. Cancer is enough of a reason to explain this. My tears are always near yet I don't always have a heavy heart. It's too hard for me to explain this fact about me.

My first operation was over twelve years ago, shortly after I fell on the floor after my ballet performance on that stage that has always taught me to love myself more. I was seven and the upset is still as I feel today. My first operation was not long after I saw the closest people to me falling apart, even the strongest of them were shaking from fear, and the ones who were always far from me were holding me dear.

My first operation was in June, I think. I'm not sure. I know that it took place right when summer came. I was in the hospital for so many hours. All my family was there, even the people that I never knew before that day. They only came because the word 'cancer' scared them. The word 'cancer' breaks so many hearts when it's related to a child.

I saw my mother's friends standing in every corner of the hospital. I saw my father's ex-wife for the first time, cousins who don't even live here. Two of my teachers were here too.

"What the hell is wrong with all of them?" I shouted to myself silently. It wasn't like I had died. It wasn't like I was dying in a few days. I still had a life to live. I still had days to count. They made me think that cancer is a big deal. I started to understand at that point that the way we perceive things is based on the idea we make of them. We choose the value we give to everything.

I did not have any precise image formed in my mind of the situation I was put in but as a naïve child, the word 'hospital' was enough to stop me sleeping at night. It's ironic because I had no idea what a hospital looked like before that day. I had no doubt that I was going home after a long day, I didn't understand the plot twist: I was going to spend some nights there. I was in the lobby, if they even call it a lobby, somewhat alone, even with all the people surrounding me. There were four brown leather couches. I can recall the picture very well, they were very old, just like the ones your grandmother could have had in her childhood house years before. I was sitting in the corner of the third couch, the one nearest to the corridor. I was lonely in my corner, resting my hand on the armrest, and my head on my arm. Too many things were on my mind. I don't know exactly what... I just didn't want to die.

The energy speaks louder than my thoughts, they are ready to say goodbye to their favorite soul.

My grandmother wasn't ready to see me leave. She was right next to me. I still see the picture of her. I still see her at that place every time I close my eyes and bring back that day.

Someone interrupted my thinking. I hate when they don't knock first. When someone comes in at the wrong timing in my mind, the story changes, and reality disturbs the scene. My grandmother died a very long time ago. Now you know the secret, now you understand why I imagine her next to me.

"Rose!"

"I don't want anyone to talk to me today."

"Your phone..."

I interrupted my sister. I didn't even want to know who was calling.

"It's Louis," she whispered while walking back to her room.

I will call him back, obviously. Not now, or wait, I will call him right away. I took my phone after she left it on the floor next to my room door and dialed his number. I hung up right after it started ringing. I changed my mind again. I don't want to talk to him now. I went to sit down on my chair. I had a chair, and a pink couch in the corner of my room. This chair was my naughty chair as a child. Now it's my grieving chair, the chair that knows all of my tears so well. He called me. Louis treats me like a child. I don't understand why he always makes sure that I'm fine.

This is unbearable. My tears! I'm not good at expressing my feelings. All I know is that I feel everything very deeply.

He called again, I had to pick up the phone. I didn't say much. The phone wasn't even on my ear. I was just holding it, waiting for him to let his words out.

"I can't believe I'm finally able to find you!"
"Very funny... what do you want from me?"
"What are you wearing tonight?"
"I'm not!"
"Excuse me, Rose?"
"I'm not wearing anything!"

He didn't understand what I meant. It was already 1pm. The party starts at nine. Everyone had their outfits picked months ago, and I'm here, standing all alone in my room, making Louis believe that I'll be there "not wearing anything".

"Are you drunk already?"

"You're just dumb, it means that I'm not going."

"What's wrong with you, Rose?"

I didn't want to answer that question. I hated when people tried to understand what was wrong with me. I never liked anyone to have an image of anything that was happening in my mind. I like to be mysterious, it makes me feel good about myself. I left Louis just like this. If he calls again I will probably pretend to be asleep. I sometimes think that Louis has a ghost that watches me all the time, so when I say I'll pretend to be asleep so I don't have to answer his calls, it's serious. I ran to my sister's room again, stole a pink pajama from her closet and after spitting on the floor for no reason, I bumped my head purposely against the wall and went to bed peacefully. I didn't want to sleep. I just fear ghosts. I don't want to be accused of being a liar. I don't want Louis' ghost to tell him that I secretly don't want to talk to him now. It's very hard to explain everything that happens to me, or inside of me. I never understood myself, I never knew who I really was, that's why I automatically hated anyone who tells me that they know me well, or understands me enough to know everything that happens inside of me.

My mother came back from work. She's a flight attendant most of the time, and the other times, I know nothing about her, but she surely does something else. She comes home once every week, or two. I sometimes feel like there's a secret behind this lady. Something we were never able to understand. It's not that she's mysterious, it's just that she never explains, and we never try to understand. The problem we all live with is the solution to everything else. We need to explain more, to elaborate our stories. We need to listen too, to want to understand, to know people's intentions and understand their reasons. We all have our reasons. I'm sure. It's the only thing I was ever sure of. We all have our reasons, and we never have to explain ourselves.

Someone is knocking on my door. I'm not waiting for anyone. I'm in bed. I'm hiding from Louis' ghost. Did he realize that I was trying to run away from him? Did the ghost tell Louis that I'm lying to him? What about this? What about that? Oh my God!

"Don't come in, whoever you are... I'm sleeping."
"You're not! Even if you were I would have to wake you up. I won't be sorry for it."

I hate voices who speak from behind the door. Voices scare me so much. I like to see faces while talking to people. I appreciate eye contact. I love it when I feel a certain kind of connection while talking to someone who is physically standing near me. I love the energies we deliver, and the warmth we share. I hate voices. I don't believe in voices. I need to see eyes, I need to feel hearts, I need to touch skin. I need everything that we never know anything about.

It's the girl I hated in middle school. It's her! She's the sweetest girl I have ever known. Her name is Diala. Yes,

Diala. Something out of this universe. I don't know why I hated her. It just happened. Now I love her. I'm crying alone. I'm not crying. I'm not emotionally hurt, but my eyes are letting some tears flow.

"You like my pjs?"

"I imagined you'd be lost in front of your mirror," she said while smiling.

"Can't you see that I asked you something?"

I was very annoying; I've always been as annoying, as strange, as disturbing. She tolerates me. It makes me happy.

"I like it! I might like your dress if you allow me to see it before tonight."

"I don't have a dress."

"This is very unique! Are you going to wear a jumpsuit? A two piece thing? What is it? Show me!"

"I'm good like this... good for another week."

"What about your New Year's Eve?"

"I don't have one, I'm not going anywhere."

"Are you joking?"

"Get out of my room!"

I started shouting to her face. I don't know why I'm doing this. Deep down I know I'm wrong, but I can't control myself. I've had cancer for so long, I will die soon. I might even need to commit suicide and end my life after the countdown tonight. Because if the universe will kill me anyway, I'd rather kill myself today. I've had cancer for too long. It's very hard to live with it. It's not something you get used to. It doesn't even get better. I want to be stronger than the universe that has created me.

SEVEN

Being Rose's friend for all this time surely has changed something in me. She's nothing like any human being any of us have met before. She's very similar to all the girls that you know when you look at her, but the moment you start listening to her stories, you feel like she comes from another world. I'm twenty-two years old. I've studied filmmaking. I started long before I graduated from high school. I don't credit anything for that but my passion.

Rose is my age, it disturbs me that she feels older sometimes, younger at other times. My day was very long. I haven't slept for the past two days. I've been preparing for the party, trying hard to make it better than any other party that I've hosted before. My group of friends revolves around Rose and her friends. Rose is the one everyone loves but that no one understands. She is loved because we cry when we listen to her stories, we laugh so hard about the memories we make with her. Rose is a rose, very tender and sweet. Very loving, very giving, very happily living, yet so isolated from our living. In other words, we love Rose because Rose makes a difference.

Rose told me that she has a chemotherapy session tonight. It worries me, it scares me. I don't know how to live with that. I can't accept the fact that my best friend has cancer. I went for a run. I'm running in the city all alone. I've never been athletic, but running takes everything out of my soul. It's very liberating to leave everything in a place as you run to another. I'm sending Rose a letter with my mind, that's what she used to do all the time:

"Dear Rose," I said as I continued running, and thinking at the same time. I wondered how everything in her life was going...

"Dear Rose,
It's somehow very difficult for me to understand all the words that you never say. I can't feel what you feel when you're not near me. It doesn't mean that I don't try my best. But it seems like it's more complex than my mind could ever be... Rose, I'll be waiting for you tonight. I'll see you like every time. You'll be shining in your dress, dancing and singing like a star..."

I didn't sign the letter in my mind. I just dropped the idea. I forgot the words. I forgot to continue the letter. The words faded from my mind. It happened just like this. I was overly distracted. It happens to Rose too.

I put my earphones on and started listening to music. I started imagining the party, the crowd, the countdown, and everything I'd been waiting for. It's a new year for all of us, except for Rose. We know nothing about her.

I stopped by Jamila's house on my way back home. Jamila is one of Rose's closest friends. She seemed to be getting ready for the big night, but I had to ask her again.

"How are you feeling?"
"I can't wait!"
"Everything is perfect, I'll meet you there before the party so I can show you round the place."
"I'll stop by Rose's and come."
And she left.

Jamila tends to doubt Rose's attitude sometimes. She's one of her favourite people ever, but she asks herself many questions about the way that she is and the way she does everything. It scares me too.

I didn't want to tell her anything about Rose. I wanted her to go there. She needs to try and convince Rose, because Rose needs to get out of her isolated world. I have a good feeling about this. Rose might change her mind even though she's never changed her mind before. It's not something she knows how to do. She never changed her mind from the day that I first knew her, nearly fifteen years ago, when we were together in first grade.

Rose will not show up tonight. She will be crying on her own, slowly pretending she's falling apart, until she falls apart for real. Because when you convince yourself that something is real, it starts haunting you, and you believe that you live with it.

Rose will surely break her own heart as she tries to find a relief. It's going to be very difficult to change the situation if it's always going to be the same in her mind. It's going to be very difficult to change the appearance of something when the roots make the same things grow.

I will call Rose again. I hope the ghost of her will let her change her mind. I can't imagine not spending this night with her. Everyone will be there. Our group of friends has always been the same, but we barely see each other now. It's almost only once a year. The gathering will not be complete.

Her phone rang. Once, then twice. Nobody picked up my calls.

EIGHT

Louis called me more than ten times in a row. I knew what he wanted, so I ignored him. I will tell him that I was eating, but his ghost will surely tell him that I was lying to him. I can't be accused of being a liar, so I ran to the kitchen, got out a fruit and sat down on the floor next to the fridge. I had a knife in my hand. I started looking at it intently. It might tell me something. I'm home. I'm alone. The kitchen is dark. I'm sitting in a corner, not knowing anything about what's happening in the world or to the world. I started talking to myself loudly. I started taking my mind to very strange places. It's very hard to explain.

"You are good, but your cancer is a sign that you need to go. You will never let go of your life, but your life will let go of you. Don't let it win. Let yourself win, even if it will be only once. You don't know where your trophy is."

I will go buy myself a snack. I need to get out of this place. My room is getting darker as I stay. It's not something I will ever be able to describe with words. It's not something I will be able to draw and colour in. It's colourless. It's black. It's not even black, because black is a colour. It's emptiness. It's not solitude. It's nothing at all.

My eyes are red. I'm walking up the stairs. I'm losing my breath. I don't know why I'm rushing. I have nothing to do anyway. At that point, my father came out of his room, I think, I'm not sure. I'm never sure. He held me in his arms. He told me that he was coming with me. He held my hand. I stopped crying. We went to get some snacks. The road was very long and the streets were decorated, everyone was singing. I started talking to him about my cancer. I don't want to live with cancer anymore. It kills every part of me. I don't believe that anything else can ever happen to me. I sometimes tend to lose sight because of excessive crying. I harm myself a lot. I told him a lot of things, but he didn't say a word. By the time I got back home I had forgotten what his voice sounded like.

NINE

Rose lost her father when she was eight years old. She says that she lost him one year after she got hit by cancer. She once explained to me that she got cancer right after his death. I don't know. She's never sure either. She's twenty-two now. She still lives with him in her mind. I don't know what got her to this state. She will be good — I promised myself once, and I keep my promise. I don't know how people see Rose. Some of them ignore her cancer, because they only see her tears, and that other world she occasionally lives in and some only see her cancer, so they ignore everything else about her. Most of them blame cancer for everything that she has, and everything that she does. Rose has used cancer as the green light that allowed her to do everything and anything that shouldn't be done. She doesn't understand herself anymore, but everyday, I understand her more.

TEN

My mind has been creating unreal memories for so long. I've told myself so many stories, but there's one story I will never stop telling, because it's that story that never stops touching me.

When you lose your father, you lose a part of yourself. You don't grieve on the moment, but you spend a lifetime wishing he was still here.

You know… I'm not sure that you do know. You will relate to what I say, you will understand me, I'm sure, but you will never feel the way that I feel, because we all feel the same emotions differently.

When you lose your father, I don't know what happens afterwards… I just know that your heart is never the same anymore, a huge part of it goes somewhere you'll never know. When you lose your father at a very young age, you don't grieve on the moment, but keep secretly grieving for so long afterwards.

Losing my father has taught me that the feeling we have about a certain thing heals when we come to terms with it. Accepting life the way it is was the key but I wasn't capable to accept such a loss.

What really shredded me into pieces was the fact that it happened suddenly. "You know," I whispered to the Rose inside of me, "I never had the chance to say goodbye. Maybe if I'd been expecting such a goodbye, I would have had at least told the Rose of me to be prepared. I never knew when the last time was..."

I had to make an end to everything, I had to tell myself that every moment was the last memory we were ever going to make together. I think that what hurts the most is the fact that in that flow of my mind, in that flow that is only made of the memories that I recall and the moments I live for, no more memories will ever be made with him.

My father. His death.

It didn't really hit me at first, it was very hard for me to believe that that last week's goodnight kiss was the last one ever. Until this day, I never let anyone kiss me goodnight, not even my mother, and never my boyfriend. I still believe that this kiss can be felt on my forehead. I never want another one to replace it. I didn't know that when he drove me back home from school it was going to be our last car ride together. The problem is that we never know when the last time is, we never say goodbye, and I never said goodbye to him. It gets harder as I grow up. I need the father every girl relies on. Sometimes I secretly envy girls who get to have dinner with their fathers, I secretly cry when I look at the pictures I hung on my wall. I have pictures of my father everywhere, even on my hospital room's wall.

It still feels like yesterday.

When you lose your father, anyone you lose after that will never be a loss. When you lose your father, you grieve for so long, you shut down, and you start having a world of your own where he still exists. When you lose your father, you will hold your phone and remember that he left not long ago, so you'll end up texting him goodbye. And you burst into tears alone at night.

The Rose of me talked as I was trying to hold my tears, "When you lose your father, you keep pictures of him everywhere. You write him a letter and you leave it somewhere in his room. It doesn't get easier no matter how long it has been since you buried him and buried your heart with him too. It doesn't get easier, but you start healing when you accept the fact that he's not here anymore."

69

People think that I have forgotten the pain, that I went through it, moved on and that I live today, in another way. No, nostalgia breaks my heart every night; I still hear his voice. I dream of him visiting me in the hospital and following up on any improvement. I always imagine the day I will run to him, hang on his neck and tell him that I have made it, that I was stronger than cancer.

When you lose your father at a young age, it's hard not to think that he might be coming back. It's hard to talk about him to your friends without falling in their arms weeping about your loss. It's hard to 'stay strong' like they always say.

I am very emotional, I am very sensitive too. It doesn't get easier with time and as I grow, the amount of tears I am able to cry grows with me. Our heart keeps breaking with time because we keep imaging the moments we could have been having. Our imagination takes us somewhere where life is colourful with the presence of this person. It doesn't get better. It kills you even more.

We live in a society of liars. We live in a society where the strongest people are the ones who are the best at hiding how they feel. We live in a society where we always feel the need to run from our emotions, to hide our thoughts, and never speak our minds. It's very unfair to have to filter your thoughts so many times before getting them out loud, they are not your thoughts anymore if you do so. I love genuine people, the ones who say whatever comes to their minds. I hate people who only care about whatever others will think of them.

Asides from having phone calls every once in a while from people who never liked me before I had cancer, there is nothing I really know about fake people. They hated me before but now they call me to see if I'm doing well. I hate them more. I hate the fact that they call me so that when my name is mentioned somewhere they can mention how much they know about my story. I hate to have to answer my phone to people who never had my number before. I don't like attention. I'm not sure... but I feel like I want to be on my own.

ELEVEN

The wind is shouting everywhere inside my room and my ghosts are screaming very loudly inside of me. I don't know if my ghosts come with the wind or if the wind comes and goes with my ghosts.

I wish, with every ghost inside my soul that it's the wind that controls my ghosts and not the ghosts who control the wind.

The wind is blowing very hard tonight, and in the world that I know, the wind blows hard when the ghosts feel alone.

Their sadness spreads all over the world.

I stand up.
I feel lost.

I take a walk.

I have to find a way to keep my ghosts happy all the time, for when they feel good, they find a way to make me feel good with them.

Their presence has a very heavy impact on the rose that I am. For they are the only creatures in this universe who understand both the rose and the girl that I am at the same time.

TWELVE

I'm alone in my room. I'm cold. I start taking my mind away from reality. I am physically here but my mind is somewhere else. I take myself to the first time I wrote a diary page; it was the only time I ever wrote about my childhood. It was a very long time ago, before life had done anything to me. I was too small sized and too small minded compared to what I believed. But here is what I wrote in my squared shaped, locked little notebook:

"Dear Diary, today was good day. Dear Diary, I see my family and when we go back I was with a lot of people in the car. I will never forget today, even if I will sleep and not write the details."

I was six or seven, maybe eight. I'm not sure if I ever had a diary, I'm not sure if I ever lived this moment, but I remember it very well. It's confusing. I wrote family without an 'i' and killed the way a phrase should be, but I thought that I did everything that could ever be done with these four lines.

I was with my family at a baptism. It was the very first time that I had gone to something like that. The church was huge, it made me feel how small we are compared to the universe. I was never like that before that day, I never really believed in the power of the universe. I never thought that we, as human beings, were the smallest part of this universe.

When I got cancer, I started understanding that life isn't everything, but it's somehow everything I want to enjoy. I wanted to heal so I could live normally. Nothing ever scared me as much as death. I guess like most people I fear the unknown, maybe it's the world that makes it too hard for us to handle. If people reacted to death in a way other than grieving and crying, maybe the image of it inside our minds would be totally different. Just another goodbye, like all the goodbyes we have to make while living. As if that person was traveling, going somewhere we know nothing about.

"The problem is the fact that we know nothing about that place," a voice whispered to me. "The death of others never scares me. My own death has always been a big deal," the voice added.

I didn't know whose voice it was, it just whispered inside of me. I couldn't recognize it, but it was surely the voice of a dead person that was trying to help me understand the situation. "The death of others never scares me. My own death has always been a big deal," the voice repeated from inside of me.

It only started happening to me when I lost my father. When my father started not being here anymore, everything about me and my life changed. I know that I'm not the same anymore. I don't really remember his voice, I only recall his figure because of the many pictures that my mother, and I, hung on our walls. The memories are now a bit blurred but I'm sure of what I'm saying. The strongest memory inside of us is the one related to our feelings and emotions. I remember how it felt when he was there, I remember the energy that was at home, and now that he's gone, so many of us started feeling down. This is the real change.

The first time I ever traveled with him alone, I was going to a chemotherapy session in a city that I can't recall the name of. I didn't know why I was going or what I was going to do. He just told me that we'd be spending some time together in some place, and before coming back we'd go see a doctor. I somehow understood that the main purpose of this trip was the doctor's appointment, but I denied understanding this. I even made myself believe that I was going on a long date to a place so far away with my father. How lucky could I be? I guess luckier than everyone that I know.

On that day, I runned to my mom to tell her about how happy I was to be traveling. Afterwards, I told my sister that I would get her her favorite chocolate. I even called Mrs. Diana, who has always been my friend even after she stopped being my class teacher. I was on the phone with her for nearly an hour, but at that time, I started figuring out that the trip would not be as fun as I thought it would. When I arrived to that city a car from the hotel was waiting for us, but I refused to get in it. I wanted to have a long walk.

My father couldn't refuse, his voice while talking to me was full of pity. I wasn't feeling half of what he was going through in his heart.

The next day, we had to walk to the hospital. It wasn't far from the hotel. As soon as I arrived, someone called my name and told my father that the doctor was waiting for us inside. When I got in, I found the office to be something out of this world. It was huge! I couldn't understand why they had to make such a big office. It smelled really good. It smelled like roses. I recognize the smell of roses very well, even then at a young age. The doctor had a pink couch on the side and then there was this royal desk with two chairs. On the side of this little palace, I spotted the curtains. I thought they might be more attractive than the ones I had in my room. For a moment, I couldn't understand how this place was a hospital. It was so far from looking like one. Even the doctor looked very young to be a doctor. The doctor walked halfway through the room to reach and embrace me. At that time, my father looked very happy. It was like he had found the person who could save his baby's life.

We spent less than thirty minutes with him, he understood my case pretty well, and asked for some blood tests. Before I left, he gave me a chocolate out of a very nice cartoon print jar. We said goodbye, and as I was at his door, I looked back and waved goodbye with a wide smile on my face.

When we went back to the hotel my father tucked me up in bed, then asked me what I wanted to have for dinner. Of course I had an answer.

My father left a glimpse of his soul in every corner of my heart. I need to go to bed. I feel like I've been lost in my own thoughts for a very long time. Nobody's home. I will sleep now.

THIRTEEN

The memories are coming back now, destroying every part of me like an avalanche.

His death wasn't just a part of my past, because I wake up every morning searching for the warmth of his hands.

I start crying.

My reaction destroys me more than anything else.

He dies every morning as I figure out his absence.

He dies every night as I start searching for him in the memories that we had.

His death isn't part of the past.

Those who left us still die everyday.

We miss them more as we live.

FOURTEEN

My cancer started healing long after I came back home. A year after that, and mainly after people knew about my cancer, I started a little walk in my school. Everyone had a sweatshirt or t-shirt with my name on it, almost everyone was holding a flag on which was written: 'Supporting Rose'. I felt special. I remembered how at first I never really wanted anyone to know about my story. I had lied about the reason why I always wore a beanie, I had lied about my many absences, but in the end, I understood that all I ever needed was some support from these beautiful souls.

I was so scared they would start treating me differently, even more kindly. I was so scared of anything being different, that's why I kept hiding everything that I had. Once I was wearing a wig in sixth grade, and running late to class, I bumped into one of those mean popular ninth grade blondies.

I said sorry politely and continued my way to class. All of a sudden, I found her pulling my hair and pushing me to the ground. I fell down. I cried. It didn't hurt me physically because my wig ended up in her hands, but it hurt me so much emotionally. Everyone knew about the only thing I always tried to hide. I was the only thing all the parents were talking about. My closest friends stopped being my closest friends because they were so mad that I had been hiding the truth for so long. I didn't know what to say, I didn't have anything to say but at the same time, I didn't hide anything — I just kept my weakness to myself. We all have the stories we never want to tell. I didn't want anyone to picture me as the 'cancer fighter who is struggling to survive' in their minds.

I must say that we are as similar yet as different as anything could ever be. Maybe our differences make us similar, or our similarities make us different. I don't know, I have my story in the hearts of so many other people, but I have never seen the same details.

I once met another girl named Rose. The first thing on my mind was that she might be a rose like me, but she wasn't. The only similarity between the two of us was our name and the idea we had of our name. I loved my name so much more than she did, simply because in a way it reflects who I am.

I'm going back to my hospital room. I'm hiding under the bed. I'm laughing. I'm hearing the sound of my laughter. I'm under the bed. I'm hiding from the nurse. Mrs. Tia will come in very soon. She will start wishing me a happy New Year. Someone is at my door again.

I didn't say a word. I think that if I don't answer, they might think that I'm not here. It is Jamila. She opens the door quietly, then sits on my bed. She starts searching for me, shouting my name, but I don't answer her. She goes outside to find my mother. She finds her standing in the living room. She tells her that she can't find me. My mother rushes to my room, searches for me in the bathroom. I am shaking. I don't have the words to talk about my situation. I don't want Jamila to come to me. She feels responsible for my grief. She blames herself for not being able to make me feel better, but I'm too hard to handle. I know myself. I stay under my bed for a while. My mother starts screaming in the house. I realize that I'm not in the hospital. I have to run to the hospital. I appear suddenly, holding my blanket, I run to the door. "I'm going, I'm going," I tell myself out loud.

My mother had been happy in the morning, she was trying to celebrate her New Year, but when you have a daughter like me, you barely see the light. I left her crying, and I left home. I had a very long walk, I started thinking about everything and anything that could possibly be thought of. I knew where I wanted to take myself. I knew a lot of things about the world. My problem was somehow bigger than all of this: I didn't know what I wanted, but I knew what I didn't want.

I arrived to a random hospital and went in. I was crying. I asked for Tia, but they told me that they didn't know anyone called Tia in that place. I started yelling, accusing them of not wanting me to feel better. I fell on the floor. Someone took me by the hand. I woke up in an office.

"My name is Adam."

"I didn't ask you."

"May I allow myself to know your name?"

"Rose."

"Are you okay?"

"Cancer…"

"I'm sorry."

"It gets better, don't worry about me."

***

Rose thinks that I don't know her. I know everything about her. I'm a therapist. I introduced myself to her today for the first time. I follow her everywhere, I've followed her case for a very long time. She's twenty-two years old, but she's stuck at being seven. She's been living in the dark for years. How can we ever explain this? I know she doesn't have cancer. I know she lives with cancer. She lives with the idea of cancer. Rose schedules her chemotherapy sessions. She visits cancer hospitals and talks about the first day she was diagnosed with cancer.

Rose will be my biggest challenge. You can't even convince her that her mind goes in the wrong directions. You can't tell her anything. I've never been in contact with her before this day but when we talked in the hospital, she seemed very calm, and defined. In that moment I doubted all that her mother has told me about her. This can't be someone who is psychologically unstable.

The first time is never real. The first impression is a big lie, because what matters is the lasting impression. The first time, you don't necessarily give a picture of who you are, but of the way you feel. The lasting impression is a challenge, because you're never sure of knowing how to keep it the same. My first impression of Rose was one of her good side. She was very calm. But the picture I have of her ruined it all. I've been following Rose to understand her case more. I think it's better if I slowly walk into her life as everything she ever dreamed of. We started talking about her. She opened up to me easily. She started talking to me about the people in her life, her group of friends, her list of ex friends, and her idea of the word "ex" in her life. Rose turned out to have an ex-life: the life she used to live and doesn't live anymore.

***

I started talking to Adam about a lot of things, I'm glad I wasn't feeling good in the morning, I'm glad I ran to the hospital. I don't know how he found me, I don't know why he started talking to me. I don't have a reason. He has his reasons, I believe. I don't have to ask him anything, I don't have to know it all. Something is very unique about this human being. I talked to him for a long time. He's going to Louis' party, it doesn't tell me anything new. I will not change my mind. I don't feel ready for anything. I wish I could start my New Year in a better way. I wish I was good enough to live my life like everyone my age. Fifteen years of cancer were enough for me. I don't think that anything will ever feel as real.

I started talking to Adam about the things we lose, the things we gain and everything that happens to us in between. I told him a lot. I revealed a lot about myself. I didn't cry in between. I was able to hold myself. I was able to control my emotions. Today will be good, I believe.

"I need to leave," I said unexpectedly.
"Can I drive you home?"
"You don't know where I live!"
"You can lead me."
"I don't remember, I will keep walking until I find the building."
"May I allow myself…"

I didn't give Adam the chance to continue. He may not allow himself to walk me home. He may not drive me home. He should thank God that I let him talk to me. Adam was just someone I met today but he reminded me of so many people that I already know. I stood up slowly because my bones were somehow hurting and after moving the curls of my hair from one side to another I put my hand in the pockets of my hoodie. I started walking tentatively to my house. It took me time to cross the street because I was very slow, and I didn't have my crutches. It was almost four in the afternoon. The party was starting in a few hours, my grief would also start in the same few hours. I was planning in my head the way I was going to break down and cry when I am all alone in my room at night. I was trying to see it like a movie in my mind, but the pictures of the party didn't want to dissolve from my brain. Something inside of me wanted me to go, but I always feel very uncomfortable around people. I hate when people start asking me about my health. I don't know why everyone is concerned. I don't appreciate when they start telling me that short hair looks very good on me. They start questioning my reasons, they start looking at me like I'm the star of the night, then when they go home, they text me saying that they were very happy to see me. The thing is that they never plan to see me.

Cancer has broken everything in me. I once shaved my head completely. I didn't want to lose my hair because of chemotherapy. I wanted to be stronger than it. I think that it's much more relieving when you harm yourself than when anything in the world harms you. So when I feel that something bad is about to happen to me, I make it happen myself, so I can always be in control. I think that if one day I start feeling that cancer is too tough for my life to handle, I'll be ending my life by myself, before the universe does it for me.

FIFTEEN

The squad will be complete tonight, but there's no need to have a full house, even if we love each other that much. We've been together since pre-school. We have lived everything together. We have spent our sleepless exam nights at each other's houses, celebrated every single birthday we can remember together, we have traveled together, we have even attended the deaths and funerals of most of our family members together. We are that group of friends that has never changed. It gets boring at a certain point, it gets stranger as we grow up, and it's sometimes annoying for me. At some point I needed people who didn't know every detail about me. I wanted to get to know people for the first time. I wanted that glimpse of happiness that comes with new people; the mystery that comes with new people. These people know everything about me. They know my stories, and the stories of every one that I know. They even know the stories that I never told. It scares me sometimes, because I can't hide from them without them knowing why I've been away. They will guess. At least, one of them will guess, and all of the rest will know. But it can also be liberating to know that you always have people behind you. It's very comforting to know that you'll always be included in their plans even if they don't mention it. Tonight will be hard, the nine of them will certainly pass by my house. They'll find me somewhere, lost between my cancer pills, my hair growth ones, and my vitamins. They will try to understand, but they will give up on me, or I will give up on them, and on myself, so I will have to promise that I'll run to the party after they leave my house.

I run to my room again, I find Jamila inside. She was waiting for me to come back from wherever I was. She has her makeup done already. It's five in the afternoon. She's beautiful. I can't even imagine how someone can look that good. I am quiet. I don't say a word. She sits on my bed. I have nothing to tell her. I get out a piece of paper and start sketching random figures. She can't understand what I'm doing, but she watches. She doesn't comment.

"You don't look as excited as you're supposed to be," she tells me while holding my right hand.
"I'm excited... I'm excited because you're excited!" I reply while slipping out my hand from hers.

She wants to take me with her, but I'm a mess. I can't go out of my room. I lost my crutches this morning. I dropped them somewhere, I think I threw them out of the window, I didn't have a reason to do that, but I did. I don't want to tell her that. She's very old in her mind, she would want to talk to my mother about it, she will over analyze it, and my mother will surely worry more about me. I hate when people worry about me, because I never worry about myself in the first place. It's good. Everything that I do is good enough to keep me safe.

I've lost my mind, I'm sure. I've been dancing around to silence in my room. The music is inside my mind. Jamila is watching a scene. It's wonderful, she loves it, she loves me. I stop all of a sudden when I remember the time I saw Jamila in the hospital waiting for her boyfriend to get out of the hospital room. At that time, Jamila was younger than me, she's still younger than me, but she's so mature that it makes it very hard to believe. If there are two things that I can't stop hating in my life, it's without a single doubt the days I spent at the hospital, and the days I spend remembering the other days that I spent at the hospital. The idea of the place scares me more than any other thing. But Jamila is here and everything is good.

I was walking slowly out of my hospital room. It was a long time ago. Mateo was living my story. He had cancer too. I was hit in my bones, but his case made him stay longer in this place because he had leukemia. He's doing much better than I am. He's going to the party tonight. He doesn't really live with cancer. It's just something that hides somewhere inside of him. I have never seen anyone less affected than he is. It's very weird, very unusual. I think he got used to it. But no, you don't get used to anything like this, because the least it does to you, is change the idea you have of your own life.

It was years ago but I remember it like it was yesterday. I was leaning on the wall next to the operation room. Jamila was sitting next to me. We didn't talk about anything related to the situation we were in. She started talking to me about her family, and her grandmother. I would have never guessed that this girl is Syrian. She can't be Syrian, she looks like us. She looks like Savannah, a little bit. Straight hair, and blue eyes. They're both a size zero. Jamila has just finished her last semester in college. She was studying music. Her voice is magical.

For all that time, I was lost in my thoughts, and Jamila lost in hers, I don't know what was going on in her mind, but surely less than what was going on in mine.

"Rose!"
"I'm craving…"
"Do I order pizza for the both of us?"
"Can we go to any restaurant near here?"
"This is a better idea."

I was feeling much better. I didn't see Jamila texting the rest of our friends because I rushed to the bathroom and spent nearly half an hour trying to control my hair. My curls are the reason why everyone knows that I'm a mess. They're good, but crazy. Jamila told everyone to meet us there. It was 6pm, the party was in three hours. I think she planned that we eat and go together so I knew everyone would come ready for the party. I was wearing a black hoodie, and jeans. I took my medicine, made sure that I didn't look sick, covered my dark circles, smiled, and went down without saying a single word. We got in Jamila's car, but I refused to put my seatbelt on. She didn't argue. As she turned the engine on, I took the AUX cable peacefully, put on calm music, and I started singing. If there's one thing that makes me feel good about myself, it's surely the way I let everything out in lyrics. While we were driving on the highway, I spotted Mateo's car. I wasn't sure if he was inside, but I think it was his car. I looked in front of me. I was calm, I started thinking about everyone that I knew. At that time I understood that we don't receive wisdom as we live, but we discover the wisdom that we have. I needed to discover this inside of me. I needed someone to enlighten me with my own wisdom. I'll be wise, I'll be good, when my cancer heals. I'll be good when I start forgetting half of what has happened to me, but my memory is stronger than me. "Jamila?" But Jamila didn't answer me. I didn't bother repeating. Maybe she's lost in her thoughts like me.

SIXTEEN

I don't know where Rose is. I'm trying to set the place with her favorite flowers. I've been here for over six hours now. The party is starting in three hours. I'll be the one she runs to right after she steps in. The lights are perfectly set, I'm almost done checking the speakers. The bar is ready, the cocktail selection is beyond anyone's imagination. This party will surely mark the year. It's a new year. We have to celebrate, in order to remember, in order to forget, because when you forget and remember at the same time, you will find a kind of comfort you knew nothing about before. I want to remember everything that made me smile, but also everything that made me cry. I want to remember everything, and be able to not feel the same way about it. I want the memories I have to be nothing but pictures that come and go in my mind. I don't want to let them control me. I don't want what's inside my mind to get to my heart. I don't want to be like Rose. I want her to run to me, and shout, "Louis help me!" without me knowing deep inside that I can't help her because my tears are as close as hers. Rose has always been the closest person to me. She has always been that human being who knows me like she knows herself, maybe better than she knows herself. She's everything I ever wanted, but she's only a friend.

My ex-girlfriend will be here tonight. I didn't invite her, but I know that she's coming. I know that she will catch my eye suddenly while everyone is dancing, then she'll look away and pretend that she never knew me. I know that she's hurt but I miss her more than I ever did. I tried to stay away from her, because I needed to detach myself from her energy. We started dating years ago, and it's been five years since we last talked.

A part of my heart misses her and I can't wait to see her tonight, but the other part hopes she doesn't show up, because I won't be acting like myself. It will be hard. I will get drunk, hug her, and cry.

"Excuse me, Louis, we need you for a quick sound check!"
"Mr. DJ!" some other guy shouts.
"I'm ready!" I say loudly.

My team is a hardworking one. They know exactly what to do, and when to do it. They know everything that I never knew. I've always been a big fan of parties. Now that I started organizing some, the excitement is uncontrollable. I will call

Jamila, because if I call Rose, she might not answer me. I don't want to ask her if she's coming, I want to tell her that Nina is coming. I don't know what to do.

"Hey, Jamila."
"Hey! You're on loudspeaker take care..."
"Who are you with?"
"Rose."
"Perfect! Rose, can you hear me?"

***

I didn't answer him. I was exhausted. I didn't want to talk to anyone at that time. He started telling me what he had, he knew that I was listening anyway.

"You don't have to come tonight, but Nina is coming. It's scaring me, I don't know how the night will go, I hate her but I'm still in love with her."
"Where are you?"
"Preparing for the party."
"I'm coming!"

I looked at Jamila and told her to drive me to where Louis was. I looked very depressed, but making him feel better would surely make me feel better too. I arrived, and by the time I got there, everything was ready. The place was beautiful. I would have never imagined that it would be looking like this. It was full of white roses, lit by various lights, even the bar was decorated. The high tables were on both sides, leaving the middle for the dance floor. I was hypnotized. This Nina would regret leaving Louis the minute she sees what he is capable of doing. Accomplishments are attractive. What someone is capable of is attractive. I don't think that anything is as attractive as success. Love is never measured by the ability of achieving. Love is not measured. It just happens, it's very unfair, very wrong, even when it feels very right. Love is every promise you break for the other person, everything they don't deserve that you do for them. "Love is wicked," the Rose inside of me told me. "Love is wicked", I heard inside me. But love is a choice. It's not only some emotions that make us happy. We surely decide to be in love with that person we choose and the story follows...

"Thank you for being here."

"She's going to show up with a group of people that you don't even know. She might act like she doesn't even know you, or she might just come and say hi."

"That's not fine with me, because I will keep remembering how we used to be."

"Then remember."

"Rose?"

"Because she remembers too. She just hides it all. I promise you that she misses you. But everything that you had is lost. So get lost. Or move on."

"Impressive."

"I need to go, I'm having a very late lunch now."

"Can you also have a very, very late party?"

"I'll try… Promise."

I hugged him and ran back to Jamila's car so we could finally have lunch. It was getting late. Night was almost here. The sky would be dark but we'd still be good. We went to a very fancy restaurant, even if I didn't look fancy at all. We sat down at a twelve seater table. I didn't ask why, it was fine by me, because I was leaning on the window. I had my world outside while Jamila was struggling to start a conversation with me. A few seconds later, the other eight human beings that I call my bunch of friends came in, and without saying a word, found their places around the table. It makes me happy. I'm always happy when I'm around people, because I tend to forget about everything. Sometimes I shut down all of a sudden, without saying a word, and it seems very weird for everyone around me. I think that everyone who never tried understanding me, never loved me. I know that I'm lovable. We all are lovable when we show the most authentic side of who we are. There's something in my heart that makes me attached to people, but also makes people attached to me. People either hate me or love me, never in between, never both at the same time. I was starting to overthink again but a waiter came and gave me a glass of red wine. It has always been my favorite. I hadn't ordered anything but obviously Tia had as she came in.

"I'm almost drunk," she told us.
"Where were you guys?" Jamila asked her.
"I don't remember," she replied.

"We were at my place, everyone's happy place…"

I don't look at the person who is talking. This is the voice of someone that I know very well. I'm having some trouble associating voices with faces. I will not look. I will keep forcing myself to remember. It's very difficult to recognize something familiar to you, but to not be able to know exactly what it is. I will force myself, there is no way other than that.

"We were at my place, we started the party," the voice added.

"We have to leave in a few minutes, Louis is waiting for us."

This group of friends is very similar. As someone who's a part of them, I have always felt the difference, but now that I've been distant for a long time I understand more. They are more alike than they'll ever realize. Everything about them makes them nearly the same. I might be like them too, but I will never know. They all have their very own stories, they all have what makes them different, but after all, their differences make them similar.

Jamila drove me back to my place then she went back to see Louis. The way back home was very crowded, it's like everyone is looking for a place to celebrate.

SEVENTEEN

I am alone in my room again. I am walking in circles, I'm not going anywhere, not even with my thoughts. I have tears inside of me. I'm holding everything carefully inside. Someone is crawling out from under my bed, someone else is coming from behind the curtains. They're people that I know, I'm sure, but I don't know who they are. The walls of my room are changing colors, I can see this. My eyes never lie to me. The couch is turning white, it was pink all my life. I don't know. "Ahh!" I scream.

Nobody's home. Everyone left. It's New Year's Eve. I'm supposed to be here. I think there's a ghost somewhere inside this house, or inside of me. Hopefully not inside of me, because I can't run away from myself. I have to scare the ghost. He has to fade away. I also have to kill him, because if I don't kill him, he will kill me.

I think life happens the same way. What you don't run after, runs after you. What you don't catch, catches you. Be in control, always. Because if you don't control your life, someone else will control it for you, and if nobody controls your life, the universe will. The universe is more powerful than any power inside any one of us. The universe made us, the universe has given us all that we have, how can we still give ourselves the right to question its power over us? Sometimes we don't make things happen, but some things make other things inside of us happen as they happen to us. They trigger thoughts, ideas, memories, moments and even actions inside of us. I couldn't control my cancer, I couldn't make it heal faster but something was wrong. Something was wrong with the way everything was so right.

As I lived, I learned that there are two types of people when dealing with life's worries: people who slowly take everything out until it heals, and people who slowly tuck it all in until it fades. But as long as it's inside, it comes back one day. People who lie to others and people who lie to themselves, people who kill others in order to stay alive and people who kill themselves in order to make others feel alive. People who think that life is either one thing or another not the two things at once, not someone in between or something that is so different from what they see. People who believe in black or white, people who only see black or white so that they are unable to understand that if we put them together we get gray, and that we always have other colors to look at. The rainbow is originally white. It disperses into seven colors, and among these seven colors one surely represents you and your situation. It just takes time to understand that blue, pink and purple can be shades of white, it takes time to understand that life isn't a matter of black and white.

After all, I'm a Rose. I'm too tender to be strong in the world. I'm too beautiful to see that someone else is ugly. My world revolves around seeing souls. People are like flowers to me, maybe plants when they're less tender than me. But even the cactus has a good side as long as you're standing in the right place. A piece of nature that is beautiful to the eye yet only keeps its beauty when it remains untouched.

EIGHTEEN

The idea we have of a thing is more powerful than how the thing really is. "Life is idea," the Rose inside of me told me.

The Rose...

The Rose inside of me is never wrong. Life is all about the ideas we have of everything. We start believing the person that we show. We start believing that the Rose we hide might have easily died and faded with time.

"Our beliefs either hold us together or make us slowly fall apart."

If we're afraid, if we're uncomfortable, if we're anything, if we're everything, it's because something inside of us has given us this idea or feeling in the first place. Our souls believe what we believe in. Every "I think he hates me", every "she doesn't want to see me" is real.

The way we are to each other is because of the way we think of each other. There's a reason behind every awkwardness that is born 'without any reason'. There's a reason behind every feeling, every emotion that we send or receive. It's either the energies our bodies and souls deliver or the interpretation that we make or fail to make.

The Rose inside of me feels to see the reality of the moments the universe shares with her.

The Rose inside of me saves me from every therapy.

The Rose inside of me could easily be another me…

NINETEEN

At first my ghosts weren't sure if there was a cure for the way that I am. I cry a lot and the way that I'm feeling becomes monstrous. They were unsure if the universe was ever going to heal me, so they decided to hunt me more.

So now my ghosts are always inside of me, and they always talk to me. I always hear them, even when they are forced to whisper to my ears.

There's a force hidden beneath who we are, a certain kind of power that never stops leading us. There's this ghost that never goes away, and this other ghost that had once took an oath to stay.

I wish they would go away, but I can't live without them inside of me. They accompany my solitude and they ease my pain. They understand my anxiety and always believe what I say.

How wicked could this universe be for giving me ghosts that I love more than its people.

I can't even think on my own now, because their voices always hear me. I was so abandoned that I felt relieved when they came.

But now all I ever know is that I miss the freedom that my solitude helped me gain.

TWENTY

I can't stay where I am. I will end up destroying the place, or it will end up destroying the person that I am. I will figure out later, I will understand later. Right now I have to go. I need to leave this house. I don't know if I should go back to the hospital or walk to the party and see what happens to me.

It's 8pm. The party starts in an hour. I'll be late. I don't look like someone who can party. I don't look like someone who can listen to music, dance or sing. I change into a black dress, start applying makeup, get into my favorite black high heels, grab my crutches, and go down. I don't want to drive. I want my bones to hurt. I want to feel the cancer inside of me. I want everything to happen to me, because if I'm hurt before the party, I'll be happy there.

I'm going to see everyone I have ever known. I will not only see the people I have never stopped missing, but also, the ones that I have never missed.

We are unfair. As human beings, we lack logic. We love what we're supposed to hate, and hate what we're supposed to love. We walk in the wrong directions, always. We never know what we're doing, and if we know, we lose sight halfway. If you have something, you'll leave it on the shelf. If the shelf is empty, you'll want to fill it. When someone makes you feel a certain kind of sorrow, you search for someone you can hurt the same way. You like to feel powerful. You define power the wrong way. Something is wrong with the world. Something has always been wrong with me, but I'm good compared to the world. I go in every possible direction and its opposite. I come back. I hate some people for no reason. I start hating people at very particular moments of their character displays. Some people are only made to be known to a very certain extent or for a certain time period. You don't have to dig deep inside of them. Other people seem very superficial, you only start appreciating who they are once they're very close to your heart.

I arrived. I saw everyone.

"Get out everyone, I missed you!"
"Rose!"
"Rosie!"
"Rosa"
Everyone had a name for me. The ten of us embraced in one big group hug. I was in the middle. They were squeezing me, I was very happy. Hardly anyone was there yet. It seemed

like one of those parties we had when we were younger. It's only the ten of us, leaving the world behind.

"Why are you guys so late?" Mateo asked us.
"It's only 8 o'clock... We still have hours to spend together," Naomi replied.
"Who's on your list, Louis?" Jade asked.
"Everyone that you know and don't know," I answered.

***

I'd invited everyone. Rose didn't know that. She thought that it wasn't going to be such a big gathering. I kept searching for a way to contact Dr. Alex but it seems like he doesn't belong to this reality. She has always told me about him, always said that he's the one who discovered her cancer, the one who kept checking up on her when she was all alone in her hospital room. She told me that he was a very gifted surgeon. I never saw him, but I know him. He's one of those people that I know very well without ever meeting. Rose's stories seem so authentic. I will surely ask her about him. It's driving me crazy. I contacted all the hospitals that might have welcomed Rose one day, and at the end of every phone call a different voice would tell me, "We're sorry, but we don't know who you're talking about." There's a secret behind this story, there's a secret that only Rose knows. As her very close friends, we always tend to question everything she is, and everything she does. It's always suspicious, it's always out of this world. Rose is very open about herself, but we don't know anything about her.

It was time for the party to start. I walked towards the DJ, held the microphone, and I suddenly found all the lights on me.

"Thank you for being here."
"Very funny, you couldn't wait for the crowd to be here so you'd thank us in front of them?" Naomi started showing her childish attitude.
I didn't say a word, I didn't comment. I was very happy to let anything affect my mood. I continued my words, "Rose!"

She looked at me, and smiled discreetly. She has a very unique smile that speaks a lot of words at the same time. She's beautiful when you look at her from a distance. She's like art. You will never understand her. She thinks she's very simple, she thinks she's very easy to be understood, but little does she know about the minds of others when it comes to thinking of her.

Rose had actually changed her mind, she'd shown up. She never changes her mind. I can't find an explanation to what she had just done. She left her crutches under the table and she was walking all around the place. I have never seen someone so happy. She took the microphone and started singing a song. By the time her song was over, more people were starting to arrive. Rose disappeared. Nobody knows where she is.

PART TWO: THE PARTY

"Only a few are special to us," the rose inside of me told me.
"Only a few make us feel alive," my ghost added.
But they're all here. I don't know how it will make me feel.

TWENTY-ONE

I hate crowds. They make me feel bad about myself, and the world. I ran away. I don't know where I'm going. I took off my shoes, wiped away my lipstick and untied my hair. I'm back with my mess. I'm going home. I pray to God that I arrive before one of them catches me and tries to take me back to the party. I'm never good enough. I'm never good. I'm always wanting to be better and I end up being nothing at all. I'm always distracted. I'm searching for so many things that I don't even find one. I'm torn between who I really am and who I think I am. Who I really love and who I dream of loving. I'm lost in the gaps of life trying to reach a certain side. I question myself a lot. I'm surely someone special. I want to see myself the way others see me, at least they define who I am in a certain way. I don't even know who I am or where I am. I'm just someone, I'm just somewhere. The fact that I know that my cells control my body is somehow controlling me as a whole. I don't want to die of cancer. I don't want to end up in a hospital. I don't want all of this. I don't want to die at all. I'm searching for another life. But for now, I'm

119

searching for my way back home. When I see myself from the outside, I don't stop criticizing the person that I am, but when I talk to myself about myself, I instantly fall in love with me. I have my reasons, my reasons will change me, my reasons will help me become better.

I met a stranger on my way back home. I didn't find out his name. We talked a lot. He asked me questions, but I was too shocked to answer anything, so he answered them himself. He knew everything about me. I don't know if this is a coincidence or if he's been following me for a while. Either way, I loved his analysis.

"You know who you are. You are lost because you're too much of everything at the same time. You want everything, so you end up reaching nothing at all. You tend to not judge anything, so you're judged for being passive. You don't like judging people, because you don't appreciate it when they do the same to you. You…"

I interrupted him. I needed to know how he was speaking to me that confidently. My appearance doesn't reveal who I am. Nothing about the way I am would ever tell anyone anything about the way I feel.

"You can't know more," I said.
"My gray hair knows more than I do. My gray hair, my scars, even my voice is faded for a reason. When you're as old as me you cannot do anything but remember, and everything that I remember reminds me of something in you."

I hugged this human being, I was hypnotized. I wanted to talk to him for hours, but I was too shy to ask him to tell me more about what he knew. He was magical. I need someone with his heart in my life. I tried matching all the names that I know to his face, but I couldn't find the word that would describe him perfectly.

I began walking on again but then I changed my mind and went back to him. I wasn't letting the words that I can't speak decide my way. I wanted to have a conversation with him. I would show up without any reasons. I would tell him that I wanted to talk to him. He would sit on the pavement next to me. I have nothing to lose.

"I'm sorry."

"You're sorry?"

"I forgot to ask about your name, my mind wouldn't stop guessing, so I had to come back...I'm Rose."

"I'm Ares."

"Ares?"

"It's the God of War in the ancient Greek civilization."

"War? No! You don't look like war. You look very peaceful."

"Listen, to have my serenity, you have to experience the trouble that I lived with. I was very energetic, I was very tough on myself not on others. I wish I was more tranquil, I wish I took myself less seriously. I'm the God of War, because I was in constant conflicts with my soul. I had a very destructive war between me and myself. I got calmer a few years ago but it's too late, I only have a few years ahead of me. If I knew that the secret of happiness was hidden inside each and every one of us, I would have never destroyed my life to find it. I came to terms with myself and now I'm very honest with myself. I tell myself everything. Now I know how to deal with who I am."

"I don't know what to say."

"You don't have to say anything. I think I understand your silence."

"Ares..."

"Tell me!"

"Can I see you again?"

"Why are you asking me? Do you think I would say no? You can easily say that you want to see me again, I don't think that I'll ever refuse this."

"I... I don't know."

"None of us know, we know nothing at all. We all have trouble expressing ourselves. We all choose the wrong words to say the right things, and the right words to say the wrong things. We all hide behind some words. I wish everyone would speak their authentic hearts. I wish everyone would love to speak more, and listen more. In every corner of the world, with every second that passes, a problem is born because of the lack of communication we have. We should take more time to explain ourselves, speak our minds, and understand the minds of others. Everything gets easier once it's understood. As human beings, we tend to criticize all that we don't understand, all that seems unknown to us. If you start thinking about everything that you dislike, and everyone that you hate, you will surely realize that you never understood how they are, and the person that they are beneath what they show. If you want to love something, you have to learn it well. If you want to admire someone, you have to understand them more. Distance and time sometimes force us to be somewhere, or talk to some people. That's why I have always said that love…"

"Love is coincidence," I interrupted him.

"Coincidence?"

"Isn't this what you were going to say?"

"I can't find a better word to express what I was going to say. Our minds connect very well."

"I've known you for less than an hour now. I don't know who you'll be to me if I get to know you more."

"Why are you spending your New Year's Eve here? Where's the party? When I was your age I had a whole weekend to celebrate my New Year. Now that I'm old, I get uncomfortable when everyone around me is loud. I'd rather have a glass of wine with my wife at home. I went down to buy a bottle for the two of us, but I met you. It feels so good. You made me want to live more… You revived my youth."

I was watching him. He was like a movie to me. His beard moved as his lips spoke the words of his heart. His hair looked as thick as it must have been when he was twenty something and he passed his hand through it every once in a while as he was talking. He looks my age. It's impressive, it really is, because I might be looking his age too. I didn't say a word, I was out of words. What was I supposed to say to such a soul? My words had stopped speaking a while ago. Everything that he said struck inside of me. He continued talking.

"My wife was like you. We were dating at that time. It was nearly fifty years ago, we were your age. We were a very unusual couple. I loved her, but we broke up many times. We had a very unstable relationship at first, but every time she would leave I would be sure that she'd come back to me, because I know her very well. I promised myself that she'd be coming back to me, not for all the time that she hadn't found me near, nor for the time that she was missing me, but because half of her was missing. We've always known that we were meant to be."

"I promised myself, because I know you very well. I know you'll be coming back to me. Not for all the time that you haven't found me near, nor for the time you were missing me, but because half of you is missing. We've always known that we were meant to be," I repeated after him. I was addressing myself to the love of my life. I'd somehow be searching for him that night as the clock strikes twelve. I knew nothing about him. I'd find him soon. He's somewhere within this universe.

"No, Rose!" a voice inside of me said as I slapped myself in the middle of the street. I will not search for love, love will find me. Ares and I said together that love is coincidence. Life is also a coincidence. You're born in a certain country, you live in a city, you go to a particular school, you meet people that you never thought that you'd be meeting, you start being someone that you discover as you live. Maybe if you were in another country, city, school, college, family, you would have been another person. Maybe you would have had another circle of people in your life. Maybe you would have been in love with someone else. Maybe you would have loved someone more or less. Maybe someone would have impressed you more. Life is coincidence, because we don't get to choose anything for ourselves. Life is coincidence, because the world is limitless yet limits you in every possible way.

I continued my way back home. As I was walking I was looking behind me, smiling and waving goodbye to Ares until we lost sight of each other. What do I do now? I think everyone's searching for me to celebrate. I'll celebrate myself for meeting Ares. He's someone who speaks his mind, someone who has a mind, heart and body that connect. I see the truth in the tenderness of his words. I smiled today for the first time in a while. I smiled for real. It wasn't just in my mind.

***

"Jamila, Naomi, where's Rose?" I screamed over the music.
"She wasn't with you, Louis?"
"No, Mateo, she disappeared!"

I thought that Rose had changed her mind, but I was right when I first said that Rose never changes her mind. She said in the morning that she'd be spending her night alone. I thought she wasn't serious about it. I was wrong.

"What do we do now?"
"I'm finding my favorite drink," Naomi said.
"I'm finding my favorite girl," Jamila added.
"Too cheesy, I'm not coming with you!" I told her.

I know that by now she'll be doing something. She'll be walking the streets of our city, she'll walk until the cold gets inside her bones. She'll remember her cancer, she'll cry for a while, she'll go to her room, shut the door, and shut down.

TWENTY-TWO

Whatever this bunch of friends is thinking of my attitude right now is wrong. Meeting Ares changed me. I want to enjoy life more. I will change my life. I will change for good. I have promised the universe that has created me. I think that when you are good to the universe, the universe is good to you, when you do good to the world, the world does good to you. I decided to go back home, eat something, then do something for the night.

It's somehow harder yet easier than we think, to go through life as it goes through us. Cancer wasn't just a chapter in my life, but a life in my chapters. It was a story so long, so real and it kept coming and going for so long with me and inside of me. We so often hide and deny when we know that it is better to admit and speak. We are everything we hate in other people. We do everything we criticize people of doing. We are always nagging for not being understood, forgetting that we never even tried to understand when we had the chance. We are more alike than we'll ever realize. If we stop for a moment, we might figure out how similar our stories really are.

"You know, Rose…" Jamila said.
"What do you want from me?"
"I always liked you because I always thought that a piece of you was inside of me."

At this moment, I was a bit lost in my thoughts that I couldn't really answer Jamila. I knew that she somehow lived a part of my story, even if the difference makes her story a whole different one. She sees everything from outside. But I'm sure about the amount of pain she feels. She has always been in the hospital, always tried to heal a heart that cancer has broken. It wasn't always easy for her. She's one of those girls that anyone would easily want to open up to.

I stood still for some time, trying to figure out what exactly had changed in me. Maybe everything is always the same, and we are the ones who make the differences. A woodden box will always be a woodden box. Some people might see that it's better if they paint it and leave it in a corner, others will want to store their toys or books in it. Some people might see it as a chair, until they figure out someday how fragile it is to carry their weight.

We always form opinions of people. Our first impression usually tells us mostly about who this person will be to us, not about who they really are. And when this person does something we dislike or says a word that runs straight to the wrong place inside of us, we leave. We leave as we leave the picture of them where it first was before. I have always believed that first impressions don't matter, they don't say a thing. What matters most is the lasting impression.

I mean, everything is temporary, even the opinions we form. They're never the same after a while. Beginnings are always exciting, but so are endings sometimes. It just depends on what we are or aren't waiting for to happen. I have always tried to understand how our feelings and emotions grow or decrease inside of us. Nothing is as confusing as the feeling we have about a moment, a thing, or even a person.

"Rose?"

"No!"

"What no? I want to go watch a movie with you."

"Quoi?"

"You speak French?"

"No, I just wanted to make you feel like I do."

"How funny…Get dressed, we're going out… Pleeeeease!"

"What was the 'pleeeeease' for? It's not like you asked me and you're waiting for my reply."

"Ummm."

"Wait, I'll be ready in five, six, seven, eight, nine or ten minutes, but meanwhile, can you..."

"No, I can't."

"I was going to ask you to get me my hair growth pills from the other room whilst I jump in my sweatpants. You just need to stop interrupting me."

"Haha fine, I'm going now. No, Rose, wait... it's the biggest party in town, I'll pick your dress."

Jamila started moving one leg after the other, showing me her slow motion acting skills, and as she did her show, I couldn't stop myself from thinking how slow everything is in our lives. Everything seems to be taking time, everything is fully detailed, every story has other stories inside of it, but when we look at it as a past, it just happens like this. We are never fully able to explain the way in which something has happened to us. We never remember everything of a certain event, only certain details. We only recall moments, then we start forming the full image in our minds. We should all understand that life is made of details, that everything lies in the smallest things. We are marked by the smallest things, and controlled by the least detailed idea we have of a certain item. The smallest part of who you are is the things that you need, and the way you speak to people says that you always need a relief. The smallest part of you lies under every word that you hear, the words that you say when you don't speak, and the moments that you often don't notice. The smallest part of who you are is without a single doubt who you are as a whole. We need to realize how small we are compared to the universe that has created us — we are powerless, useless until we make ourselves useful. We should give more to the universe in order to allow it to give us more. The worst thing the universe has done to any one of us is making us think that we're as big as we can imagine. The universe is wicked, and so are our souls. We are wicked souls trapped inside some naïve hearts and happy minds. This is who we are, something we can never explain nor understand. We have to live with it.

It was 10pm at that time. The party is on fire on the other side of the street. We're only two hours away from the new year. Two hours away from the end, or the new start. I'm torn between living with everything that has happened to me in my past and everything that will be happening to me in the future. The future is ahead of us. I will focus on it. I will focus on it until something happens again and destroys every cell of my body.

"Are you ready, Rose?"
"Almost..."
"I love your hair."

My hair is the messiest thing you can ever see or touch. It's beautiful. I'm madly in love with anything that is a mess. When people are a mess, they're somehow a piece of art. When something goes to every side of the world and back, when we figure out halfway that we've been walking in circles the whole time.

"Wait..."

I grabbed my pink backpack, tucked in my pajamas, held my fluffy socks in one hand, Jamila's hand in the other and started my way down. I was calm. I had a very unlikely smile on my face. I was starting to feel the universe inside of me, I was starting to feel that I'd been making myself a victim of life for no reason. Maybe it was time for me to take the lead, to start the wars that I like and cease the ones that stop my heart from beating. We got into Jamila's car. I left my crutches on the back seat. I didn't think that I'd be needing them tonight. I think I can do the whole coming year without them. I will convince myself that I'm good enough to walk on my own. As she started driving, Louis' playlist began automatically. He'd given her a copy of the music he was playing tonight. By the time we arrived it was nearly eleven. We still had an hour remaining before the year ended. I felt I might need to spend this hour thinking and feeling everything that had happened to me, or I might need to party harder than I'd ever done. "Can't it be both?" I asked myself. I made up my mind. I would enjoy myself and forget about the world. I would think later; be mad at everything later…

"I'm so glad that you're here," a voice said.

"I regret that I came."

"I missed you."

"I started missing you the minute that I saw you."

"Tell me how you've been."

"Good, but I wonder how I will be…"

"It's been five years since we last talked."

"It still feels like yesterday," and I burst into tears and ran to the restroom.

I loved him once, he was something out of this world. I loved him more everyday. But then he left. I almost forgot all the stories that we had. Now that he came back, all the pictures came back to me with him. Every emotion was in my heart again, every giggle, every sorrow, every smile, every tear… I don't know what to do. Whilst feeling all this I was also watching Louis. He was standing at the other side of the room. Nina was near him. She had the courage to run and hug him. It was easier for him than it was for me. At least they still have stories to tell, they still have kisses to steal. They might get a second chance after today.

The only thing that remains the same over the years is the way we feel about a certain person. Love is stronger than us. We never get over someone who was once everything that we had. We can't forget the way we felt in their arms, we can't live like it never happened. We get used to the way things have become. We live with the changes that we have made. We learn to love again, we learn to love somebody else. Every time we tell ourselves that love before that person was never real. Every time we remember our previous relationships, our previous adventures, lies, moments. We start comparing every love that we had to the love that we still cry over. We compare every good thing any lover has done to us to every bad thing the love of our lives has done to us. We are only able to love once, I believe. First love, I'm not sure. Because my first love was a ghost hidden inside of me.

Our first love will always be somewhere inside of us, even long after they leave our lives. We never love the same way twice, even when we find ourselves capable of loving the same person over and over again.

He's coming back to me. I don't want to start my new year with him. I don't want our story to start again. I don't want to feel the joy that he brought to my heart again, because I'm not strong enough to grieve again like it's the first time. He's walking towards me, he's flipping his hair. He's lighting the cigarette he's holding. He's playing with his beard. I don't know if he's worried or if he's just confident. I have known him very well, years ago. Everything has changed now. I can barely recall his voice. He's different. He's like a stranger.

"I'm sorry, Rose."
"Sorry for what?"
"I miss you!"
"I need to be alone now."
"You were right when you told me that I will never find someone who will love me like you do."
"It's too late. It's too late, Dan."

He held my hand, he wanted me to dance with him. I didn't want to look him in the eyes. I wasn't able to do so. I didn't want him to hold my hand tighter than this. I didn't want to dance with him. The last time we were together was five years ago, when we were eighteen.

He used to get me flowers when we were younger. We were too young for love when we first fell for each other, we were reckless. I don't think that anyone understands what we had. I don't want to remember. I don't want to miss his touch again. I don't want to cry when I see him. I don't want to leave when he comes in somewhere. He held my hand until we reached the dance floor. Another song will be added to the list of songs that remind us of each other. He's taking the lead, he always takes the lead. The song is speaking to me, his steps are also speaking to me. With every "Darling, save the last dance for me" he pulls me closer to him. The song describes my night. It's been real, everything between us was real. We told everyone that we were never serious, that we secretly hated each other. We ran away but with every step that we took that kept us from being together, I was surely searching for him in every soul that I met, and he was searching for me in every girl that he loved. I started recalling what I was repeating after Ares a few hours ago. Ares was right when he was talking about his relationship with his wife. At this exact moment, his voice popped in my head again, and he repeated the same thing twice: "I promised myself that she'll be coming back to me, not for all the time that she hasn't found me near, nor for the time that she was missing me, but because half of her was missing. We always knew that we were meant to be". His voice was somehow faded, and old, but his words only spoke the truth.

Dan hugged me very tightly after the song was over. It felt like I was falling in love for the first time in my life. I disappeared. I made sure his eyes didn't catch mine. I didn't want to relive the same love story again. He's too much for me to handle. He's everything I have ever dreamed of, but I can't find a picture of a reality that includes him.

The night was going well for every human being in the place. The energy spoke louder than any words. The smiles were obvious. A very happy new year! I was watching Louis the whole time. He's my best friend. I need to know what he's doing at every moment. I need to be ready to take him away from Nina if she starts giving him a hard time. But I had a feeling that nothing would be going wrong tonight. I'm good. I'm good because I promised myself that I'll be good. I secretly forced myself to be good at first, but now I'm good for real. Naomi came to see me, she offered me a shot of tequila. I needed it more than I needed anything else at that time. I can't get drunk. My unconscious Rose is stronger than me, I can't let it appear now. I need to have a walk on my own. I need to feel some warmth. Naomi's here, I can't hear what she's trying to make me listen to.

"It's so good to see you!" She said.

I smiled, she smiled back, and we started dancing to the music. Louis came. He took me in one hand, took Naomi in another. He wanted us to check if the setting was still as perfect as it was at the beginning. I hadn't seen the roses that he chose. There were three hundred and sixty-four white roses, and one red one. I couldn't help but take the red rose. Roses remind Louis of me.

TWENTY-THREE

Rose was always there for me. She's been my friend for as long as I can remember. I know that she doesn't enjoy Naomi's company. She never had a reason. She just feels this way. She thinks that this is enough of a reason. We all have reasons we never understood, decisions we never took, choices we never made, and moments we never lived. We all have this life we never lived, or only lived inside of us. I don't want to think more about her, and the way she sees the people around her.

The music is loud, everyone is moving. The dance floor is full. Every flaw is covered, because every detail is unseen.

A part of us worships perfection, and hates the people who make us feel that this perfection is so far from who we are, and where we are. We worship perfection, because it can never be anything but an idea. We love the abstraction of things. We somehow worship God because we never see him, we only see the power he has over us. We need something to hang on to, and permanent power to rely on.

Perfection is the little spark that could have made every star shine brighter, every detail stand out more and every one of us be more of who they could be. We worship perfection, because we run after the unobtainable, because we think that we crave the ideal. The truth is that we are attached to our flaws, and to the flaws of others. We are attached to everything that makes our lives imperfect, because imperfection is what makes us human.

Rose is standing alone, she is smiling. I know how worried she is. I know everything that's running through her mind. She's trying to stop her mind. She's always been one of the people who constantly think. She's very intellectual, very deep sometimes.

Nina and I are having another beginning. It feels like the start of a new relationship, a new love. It's a feeling I never knew anything about before today. We're ten minutes away from the new year. Everyone is looking at the time. There's a clock projected on the wall behind the bar. It's 11:51pm. I'm having random conversations with everyone in the place. I want to make sure that everyone is having a good time.

"The time of my life," Rose whispered to my ears...

***

Yes, I was never this happy. I realized that I was always putting myself in a mould that I didn't know the shape of, I was holding myself back from doing anything and going anywhere. Now I'm at my best. I'm at my happiest. I don't care about anything that has happened to me. I have cancer, it doesn't change me. I break down and cry sometimes, it doesn't define my strength. What I have is far from being what I am. I am what I want to be. Tonight, I'm happy. It's nearly midnight. I'm almost leaving everything behind. I will have my last drink for this year, I will have my last moments. I will apologize to everyone I have secretly hated. I will secretly apologize to them. I will decide how my life will be. I will make a list of the things that I want to stop, the things that I want to pursue, the people I want to keep, and the people who are better when they're far from me. I will not do it alone, I will let everyone that I know do it with me. I will change the world. The world will be good, because I will be good.

TWENTY-FOUR

I'm waiting for the digits to move. We're only five minutes away. I'm standing alone, waiting for my good luck. I'm waiting for my newest start. I'm rising again. I will allow myself to go for one last walk. I need to feel the loneliness I have always felt. If this is a new start, I need a very old ending.

I need an ending that will match my past.

I walked slowly behind the bar, where I was hiding my pink backpack. I took it, went back to our table, took two shots of something I don't know the name of, wore my pajamas pant over my dress, took off my high heels, and started wandering around in my fluffy socks.

I went outside, looking for someone to talk to. I needed to let everything out, so I could be as clear as I could be on the inside. I was alone, no one was on the streets. I had to talk to myself, to remind myself that at the end of the day, I'm all that I have. I have to love myself, I have to put myself first. I have to understand myself, forgive myself, and come to terms with myself. I have to take some time at the end of the night to speak to the Rose inside of me about all that was good, bad, wrong, and right in my day. I have to do everything I have always been waiting for someone to do for me.

You have to do the same, everyone that I know should do the same. Maybe all of you aren't as fragile as I am. All of you aren't Roses made of petals that shut down at certain times of the year. All of you have better, or worse luck… All of you are not who I am, but you can always control your own life. You can always be grateful, ask for more, or less of the things you need or don't need in your life.

I kept walking. I didn't know where I was taking myself. I was aimless. I sat down on the pavement all alone, waiting for someone to come near me, waiting for someone to come talk to me.

Nobody's here. I feel empty. I only have five minutes left until I go back to the party.

***

On the other side of the street, we were having the time of our lives. I looked for Rose again but she's definitely not here.

144

I hope she'll be back before the countdown. Naomi is instantly more comfortable when Rose isn't around. I didn't bother asking her if she knows where Rose is. She would have just turned her head, and pretended that she never heard me, that the music was loud, that her ears only listen to one beat. I went to Nina, I hugged her without saying a word. I missed her. No amount of hugs will ever be enough tonight. I'll be asking her out again soon. I'm glad that this party united everyone that I have ever known. I once did every possible thing to be with Nina, but I ended up in the arms of another girl. I did everything to keep her close to me, but the only thing she ever did was walk farther away. Tonight she's different. She's letting herself be. I'm thankful. I'm still searching for Rose. Jamila and Mateo might know the secret of her absence. They were laughing from their hearts, they were enjoying every second of the night. It's beautiful. People are beautiful in this place. I only see beautiful souls here. I started whispering once I approached them. They were hearing me very well, but they didn't have any answer to my list of questions.

"I can't find Rose, where is she? How did she leave?"
"Louis," Jamila said.
"I can't find her, I'm worried about her. She might keep walking without having a destination. She might go back home, she might harm herself."
"Don't worry about her."
"I am worried, Jamila."

"She'll be back! I know her very well. She'll be here as the clock strikes twelve."

***

Jamila knew me well. She knew me more than I ever knew myself. I don't know how all of this is happening in five minutes. I will cry, then I will go back like I'm having the best night of my life. I started crying on my own. Adam came. He sat next to me, he started wiping away all of my tears. He stood up, held my hand, pulled me up, and started walking with me.

"Are you okay?"

"You think I'm not?"

"I don't know, I'm just asking."

"You're a therapist! You know everything… Don't act like you don't know every detail about me. Don't pretend like you found me here. I'm sure you followed me from the minute I left the party."

"I did. I had to. I promise you that I came to the party to celebrate. I didn't come to keep an eye on you. I'm sure you're good."

"What about my cancer?"

"You're good. Everything about you reveals how good you actually are. Why are you trying to destroy yourself? Why are you trying to feel bad? Nothing is wrong with you, Rose. Give yourself some time, control everything that goes through your mind, you'll be better than anyone you have ever known."

I held his hand and walked with him the whole way back. We arrived a few minutes before the countdown was due to start. I left Adam at the entrance, because I had to run to my table to take off my pants and get back in my high heels. I needed to adjust my lipstick, and wipe away the smudges of eyeliner that my tears had made. Louis was having a very serious conversation with Nina. I was standing behind them, listening to every word they were saying.

"Either come into my life, or leave. Having you hovering in and out of it disturbs me a lot. I can't handle this. No... Don't ask me to come back to you. Every piece of my heart is still as attached to you as it was years ago, every piece of my heart wants you, but my mind hates you. My mind doesn't want anything that looks like you, smells like you, or even feels like you. I'm not sorry for anything, I don't want you to be sorry for anything either. I need to be away from you, because the way I felt when I was younger is coming back to me. You're making me relive my teenage years and I don't want to."

She didn't answer him. He couldn't be wrong. Jamila and Mateo were at the other side of the room. All the lights were on Naomi as she was moving, shouting as she sang and danced. Adam was standing with someone that I had never seen. I think it was one of Louis' friends from work. Everyone was fully into the party, even the bartenders were singing along with every song. One of them looked very familiar to me. I don't know where I could have seen him before, but he looked like someone that I knew well. I remembered those eyes very well. I knew his hair, his smile, and every detail about the way he stood. It's driving me insane. Maybe I saw him in my dreams. Maybe I spotted him somewhere and brought him into my life unconsciously. I left my beer on the floor, grabbed Louis, Nina, Mateo, Jamila, Naomi, Adam and the rest of my friends by the hand and told them to follow me. It was a déjà vu. I was holding Louis' hand, who was holding Nina's in his other hand, who was holding Mateo's, and so goes the list. We were walking attached to one another until I reached the microphone. The music got turned off. I started the countdown as they were all standing behind me, holding each other's hands. They were repeating after me as I said:

"Ten!" And I looked around me.

"Nine! Eight! Seven! Six!"

"Five!" Dan said as he took the microphone from behind me.

I smiled. I continued my countdown

"Four! Three! Two!"

All smiles were obvious. The happiness was all over the place, and finally we could shout the last word in this year.

"One!" We all shouted in one microphone, letting the number stretch out.

"Happy New Year! Happy New Year!" I repeated. Dan kissed and hugged me. The last New Year's Eve we spent together had been almost seven years ago, long before we graduated from high school.

"Come here guys!" Adam said.

"This is the best group hug I've ever had," Mateo whispered with his usual half smile.

"This could possibly be a dream," I added.

"This is my dream come true," Louis said as he smiled peacefully.

TWENTY-FIVE

The music is on again. The party is louder than ever, and the night outside darker than it has ever been. The stars are shining more than the diamond rings of any girl inside. The stars are speaking to us. The universe once explained to me that the sky always has a message to tell us. The universe is happy today, and so are we. The universe gives us what it has. Tonight, the universe has love, and euphoria.

We know nothing about tomorrow. Let it remain a mystery, for the biggest mysteries hide the best surprises.

With every second of this new year's beginning I'm asking the universe with every piece of my soul to heal me from everything that I have and to give me all that has always been mine. I have a very good feeling about my life after today. I was surrounded with so many people yet felt like solitude was my only friend. I have understood that everything that I am is what I have chosen to become, that life is ours to make, after all.

151

I've had to be patient for a long time. I was never patient. I was only a patient in every hospital that I went to. A patient to each and every one of my doctors. I'm a cancer patient but I suffer mostly from what comes with my thoughts. I'm not sure. I'm torn between two worlds. I don't know if I'm depressed because I'm lonely, or lonely because I'm depressed. I don't know what's hurting me more. I don't know if it's my heart, my body, or my soul. I've been crying a lot, searching for someone to cry with, because I'm too weak to handle my tears alone. I can't calm myself. I need someone to hold me every now and then. I need someone to tell me that I'll find my way. It's alright to cry out loud, because it's alright to laugh out loud too.

I make my way back into the party. My favorite song is on. Everyone is partying hard. I'm waiting for this party to never end. I saw Naomi walking to the bathroom, I followed her.

"Why are you whispering, Rose?"

"I was grabbing your attention. I'm whispering because I want you to listen to every word that I say."

"Are you out of your mind? Can't you see how loud the music is? How can I hear you?" she said loudly.

"You'll hear me if I whisper, because we tend to want to listen to all that we can't hear. You'll make some extra effort!"

She left without saying a word. I grabbed her arm. I forced her to stay and I said, "Listen to me… tell me more about you, as a human being that I hate."

"Excuse me?"

"I'm listening to you."

"I don't think you need to know anything about me. I might allow myself to tell you about yourself."

"The ghost of me doesn't know you, and the ghost of me tells me to hate everyone that they don't know."

"Rose," Naomi smiled as she caressed my arms.

"I don't know why we never liked each other."

"I don't have anything against you, It's just that you never took the time to appreciate my presence."

"What are you? I don't even know why people like you exist. If I were you, I would have died a hundred years ago. I would have committed suicide. You know, I advise you to commit suicide, my ghost also advises you to commit suicide... like right now. Because if you don't I might force you to do so. I might kill you. So you better do it yourself."

"How dumb."

"Still not dumber than you."

"Are you trying to ruin the night?"

"I'm just trying to fix what I've ruined in your mind. We have to start accepting each other. I will force myself to accept your presence."

"What in the world have I ever done to you to make you hate me like this?"

Naomi didn't bother going to the bathroom. She walked straight to Louis and started telling him about this conversation. I knew I was in the wrong. "What the hell did you just do, Rose?" I asked myself. I didn't have any explanation. It made me laugh, at least. Some words are better left unsaid. Some ideas are better left unspoken.

When Naomi came back to the table, she looked very different. She was somehow feeling better. I knew she'd been waiting for something to break the ice between us for a long time. We were finally good.

I was feeling a lot better than I had ever felt before. The voice inside of me was appearing once more. This time it was whispering, "You think all the time. You need to detach yourself from life. You need a little goodbye, a day to spend in bed forgetting about the world you just left behind. We need to stop our thoughts, to have a little pause, to give ourselves the chance to know our hopes. I'm going home. I'll still be a Rose."

When you talk to yourself, you feel some kind of magic. You can get to terms with yourself, and with each and every one of your friends. You have no time to hate. Your soul has no room for hatred. Be indifferent. Don't think, don't care. It's alright. Don't let your emotions control you. Control your emotions, for your emotions somehow control your living.

It's only one in the morning. Nobody's drunk yet. I'm waiting for this moment. I don't want anyone to be aware of their vibrations. I'm on my own most of the time. I'm in the future, in the past too. I'm taking my mind to places I've never been to before. I'm imagining moments, recalling memories. I've mixed both of my memories and my ideas, to the point that I don't know if they're a part of my past or my future.

It was 1am. The picture of Nina and Louis standing in the middle of the party was all that I was able to see. I hate Nina. I don't hate her for who she is, but for what she does. I understand that she has a big heart. I know that she's kinder than most of the people that I know but that is covered up by all that she does. All that we are is hidden in all that we do, because we have been told that our actions are a reflection of our thoughts; that if we do good, we are good. The better we do, the better we are. I'm not sure if this is truly what defines us.

We tend to define ourselves according to our thoughts and intentions. At the end of the day, the person we are is way different from the person the others know. The problem we all live with is, without a single doubt, the problem of always labeling everything. We judge by forming opinions, never thinking that the opinions we form can easily be wrong. The problem we all live with lies within who we think we aren't and who we think people are. As human beings, we are much more than just being good or bad. We are everything we think of, everything we love, everything we hate, and every detail in between. We are everything that we feel, every word that we say at the end of the day. We shouldn't force ourselves to be something or someone. We shouldn't force the others to be who we want them to be. We should be tolerant, accepting people for who they want to be. You don't necessarily get what you give. You don't necessarily get treated the way you treat others. But when you are good, you will surely give people the urge to be good to you too… We should be kind. We should forgive more, love more, and hate less. We should work harder, and rest more. We should do everything and its opposite with everything in us. We should think well when it's time to think, so when it's time for us to sleep we can fall asleep deeply. It's okay to be everything and everyone in one soul. You can always do it all. Dedicate yourself to love yourself. Have some balance in your life. Balance is all that you need. It's okay to be one person during the day, and a completely different person at night. You might find yourself a completely different person at home and at work than you are with your friends. Everyone has a very different lasting impression of who you are. But who knows you better? They all do… We're all two souls trapped in one the body of one. We're all everything that we see in everyone else. We're everything the universe has. We're magic, I believe. We're an abstraction. We're something we can never explain, something we can also never understand, because the life we live can never be understood or explained.

TWENTY-SIX

As a Rose, I've always been hiding half of the world inside of me. Half of everything I know and believe in are in my dreams. Half of the stories that I have lived, have first happened inside my soul. I might be strange. I might be different. I feel too much. I scream too much. I'm something no one will ever understand. I think the feeling of having an illness is more disturbing than the illness itself. The idea of being different and unaware. The idea that you might be having something less or more. When you come to terms with what you have, when you come to terms with your body, and your soul, things get better. I think this is what I'll be doing starting today.

Adam was still nearby. I hoped with every piece of who I am that it wasn't to keep an eye on me.

"Why are you standing alone?"
"Why are you asking me?"
"Are you having fun?"
"I am, Adam."
"I'm glad. I'm leaving now."
"I'll see you tomorrow, come have breakfast with me."
"I will."

He hugged me and left. It was very late but I didn't feel it –
I was feeling relieved. Everything felt better than it was
before. I was grateful. Mateo came to me right after Adam left.
He has always been one of my closest friends. I'm attached to
him; to everything that he does. His stories somehow seem to
affect the way that I am. He started talking to me.

"He left?"
"Who are you talking about?"
"Him!" He said, pointing at the door.
"I can't see anyone."
"I'm talking about Adam, Rose!"
"He left."
"So, who is he?"
"He's a therapist, he's Louis' friend too."
"He was here for you?"
"No, for the party."
"You like him?"
"I don't know, Dan's here too. It's very confusing. Do you
want to…" I motioned to the bar.
"Yes. Yes, Rose! Let's have a drink."

Jamila joined us as we were walking to the bar. I asked for water. I needed something to detox my soul from everything. It had been so long since I'd drunk water.

"Just water?" the bartender asked quizzically.
"I don't know."
"Come behind here."

I laughed. I made the whole way round behind the bar and stood next to him, staring at everything silently. He took the first bottle, twisted it in the air then held it again. I smiled but my reactions weren't overly expressive. He added another bottle to his trick and with every smile of mine he would add a bottle and make his juggling more challenging. After he finished he handed me my glass of water then gave me a high five. I giggled discreetly, and left. I made the whole way back and sat at the side of the bar. Dan came. He hugged me from behind.

"I don't like back hugs."
"You like my hugs! I've missed you!" He said as he hugged me tighter.

I pushed him away. I was in a war between what I craved and what I needed. It's too late. It's too late for the good memories we made to happen again.

A part of me is telling me to keep him close again. Another part of me is sure that he'll only be around for the night. I'm too tired to believe myself. I have to call my mother. I have to wish her a Happy New Year. I hope she's not sleeping yet. I call her twice. She doesn't answer. She calls back after a few minutes. I'm standing next to the speakers. I can't hear her well. I turn the music off. Everyone looks at me like I killed someone. Their eyes kill me. I cry behind the bar. I cry for so long that I forget the deal I made with myself. Everything is coming back to me. I will not change, because people don't change. Perhaps I will be able to change when everything in my life changes. I need a new house, a new idea of home, a new idea of life. I need something to be exciting. Beginnings are exciting, but everything that comes after scares me.

Dan is still here. I don't know what to tell him. I was enjoying my night until he came near me. I need a calmer life. I need a stable life. He doesn't know anything about that. He's everywhere. I can't be with him anymore. A part of my heart knows that I will never love anyone the way that I loved him. A part of my heart knows that no heart will ever love me like his, but the other part of my heart isn't able to handle him again. A part of my heart isn't ready for the stress that comes with his love. I will have to make up my mind, because if I decide to be with him, I will go and throw myself in his arms.

TWENTY-SEVEN

Things started falling apart again. I closed my eyes for a while. The music was loud, but my sleep is deeper than any sound. My cancer was back. My bones hurt like never before.

"Where is Adam? Where is doctor Alex? Why am I here? Where's the hospital?"

Jamila was standing next to me. She knew that something was wrong again. I was hiding my tears. It's very sad when you drop a tear, after holding it for so long. She was standing next to me, without saying a word. She was making sure that nobody would come talk to me. She didn't want me to start crying or seem unhappy. I walked over to the bartender again and stood next to him for a few minutes. We shared smiles. There's something about him that makes me want to be next to him. Maybe because he doesn't care about me, maybe because he doesn't know me. Sometimes all we need is some distance, but we never find it, so we never feel better.

I want to be better.
I want to be good.

I took a deep breath. I smiled. My life will change when I apologize to everyone I've ever been wrong to. Even if it's been a while, even if they already forgave me. Spoken words change a lot. I hate the ice that separates people. I hate when things aren't natural. I hate awkwardness. I will fix things. I will make everything better. I will feel better. I will forgive everyone long before they apologize to me. We are all wrong sometimes. We're only human, our flaws are sometimes stronger than us.

The party was almost over. It was three in the morning. This was the longest I'd ever been outside my room. Dan held me in one hand and Naomi in the other. Naomi held Nina's hand who held Louis' hand who held Jamila's hand who held Mateo's hand and so goes the list until the whole crowd was literally lined up. We started singing a song. Dan had the microphone, he handed it to me, and we kept passing it on and on until everyone's voice was heard.

"No matter where you are, no matter who you are with, we will take the year you had, and give you a happy new year instead."

"We're here again, and we hear you more than ever. Your heart is bigger than it has ever been."

"It's not an end, but the beginning of another happy ever after."

"Because we'll say much more than all the words we have ever said before."

"Happy New Year, Happy New Year."

"Kiss me hard and hug me tight."

"Love me more and scream it loud."

"This year is our year! Happy. New. Year!"

"No matter where you are, no matter who you are with, we will take the year you had, and give you a happy new year instead," we finally said.

This is a piece of heaven. What we are living can't be real. While a part of me is celebrating, a part of me is with the other part of the world. While you are crying, someone else is having the time of their lives, and vice versa. So you better never compare who you are to who anyone else is, who they have to who you are with, what your life looks like and how their life is.

The music is loud again. Everyone is back in their place. Nothing is changing. Dan is coming back to me. I don't think I will push him away this time. He's done a lot to me, but the love I have for him will surely erase it all. I wish our relationship never ended, I wish our relationship never started. It's very complicated to explain. I just wish. It doesn't mean anything.

"Want to dance?"

"I'm mad at you."

"I'll kiss you."

"Don't even try."

"I will kiss you, Rose."

"I don't know."

"I'm still in love with you."

"I have to go."

"To where?"

"To a place where you're not."

As I started turning around to leave, he held my wrist aggressively and pulled me close to him. He looked me in the eyes, and kissed me. His kiss. I don't even remember his kiss. It felt like the first time. It felt like falling in love for the first time with someone I'd never known before and that was the only thing making me want to have him once more. If I remembered anything that we had, I would have cried alone again. He started slowly, he took the lead, he did it well, really well. You wouldn't want to stop kissing him, ever. I pushed him away all of a sudden. I had to leave him before he left me. I had to take the lead for once to stop kissing him before he'd had enough. I ran to Jamila and hugged her. I was out of words. Dan didn't keep me out of his sight. He smiled at Jamila. Now she knew the secret. I was lost, but Dan came again to me and we started dancing. We didn't need any words to know that we were together again.

I hope this time it's different. I hope it doesn't end as fast as the times we had when we were younger. The love we have for each other is stronger than anything else in the world, but I don't really believe in love.

"I don't believe in love," I claimed as I stood up straight in front of him.

"I don't believe you. How do you define every moment we share. If it's not love what could it be?"

I didn't reply, so he had to continue.

"We have nothing but love. We weren't able to stay committed. We destroyed every good thing in each other. We left, we came back. We said we hated each other. We started hating each other. You used to cry when you used to see me with anyone other than you. Your presence has always lingered even though you weren't mine to keep. I always wanted to share everything with you. My life revolves around you. My life revolves around who you are and what you do. If this isn't love, tell me what is! Tell me, Rose. You, who knows everything. You who just said that love doesn't exist!"

I hugged him. I didn't say a word. I had nothing to say. I'm attached to him, that's all I know. Attachment is stronger than any love. Attachment is the hardest thing to get rid of, or get over. As I let him out of my arms, the song from the beginning of the party came on again. As a Rose, I always promised to 'save the last dance' for him. The night didn't seem to be ending even though we were a few minutes away from sunrise and people were leaving one after the other. We were still standing in the middle of the dance floor, pretending we were the only two in the place. Right then the amount of happiness in me merged with the amount of happiness in him could easily make the world a happy place. This is my happy place, my happy night, and my lucky day. I had a very good feeling about this year.

"Thank you for being here," he whispered as we were dancing.

I held his hand. He grabbed it and kissed it.

"True love only comes once, Rose," he said as the voice inside of me whispered.

I didn't respond, but deep down I knew that this kind of love was very rare, because finding someone who loves you as much as you love them, finding comfort in someone is one of the hardest things in the world. But the Rose of me told me that I must let go of him anyway.

PART THREE: AFTER-PARTY

"Have you ever given up?" they said quietly inside of me.

"A hundred times, if I counted properly."

"But they say that there's something special about the way you are, they say that there's something different about your smile."

"It's something I have never explained, to give without having in the first place."

TWENTY-EIGHT

"I'll be there before you arrive."

"Thank you."

"Do you even know what I'm talking about?"

"I never know what's happening inside your mind, Dan."

"I mean, I will be at every step of your life even before you reach it. I will be at every moment, every smile, and every tear. I don't think I'll ever be able to replace you, Rose."

I sat down, pulled my leg up on the chair and rested my head on my knee. I didn't know what to say. I wanted to be with him, but I also needed my distance. We are very different. We tried to be together before and it didn't work out. I don't know what could make it happen now but I still feel him on the inside.

Something about the way I am is disturbing the way I'm living. Something about the way we all are is changing our living. The story gets real at a certain point, but the most real story that could be told is the story of the words we keep to ourselves, the words we never say.

"Your heart and his collided for a reason," the Rose inside of me started whispering. "If there's love you shouldn't worry. All the differences will make you alike. Stop being afraid of love and all that it has done to you. This time might be different... Let it be." The Rose inside of me disappeared. I tried finding her, but it seemed like she'd only come to whisper those words and leave.

Things get mixed up in our minds because we want everything at the same time, we want to draw the details before even having the borderlines. We lose our capability by craving the capability of others, we lose who we are when we start craving what others are. We fear to face, we prefer to avoid. We're secretly hurt, yet we deny how we feel, and it only hurts us more. We deny until we forget.

***

I was watching Rose from so far away. I wish she could see herself from our eyes. There's something beautiful about her. Something we can never explain. There's something about her voice when she calls my name. She screams, "Louis!" and the whole place looks at her. There's something about her character that makes her strong and tender at the same time. She's bold, there's no doubt about that, but she is also everything that is the opposite of that. I will fail to explain her life, I will fail to describe her days. I will fail to do so many things that she does. Being similar or different isn't what really unites us. There is some kind of chemistry we are made of, there is some kind of energy inside of us that either pulls us closer or pushes us further away. Anything that we know, any rule we have created, can never be applied to Rose. She has her own rules, she has her own ways. We have to treat her differently. Her family knows, her friends know, the love of her life will know. Everyone that Rose meets ends up having the secret revealed.

TWENTY-NINE

Louis was watching me from where he was standing. I could see that his eyes caught me all the time. He knows exactly what I'm thinking of. He knows that I'm split into two, because a part of me wants to be a fool while the other part of me is always steady, standing still watching how the world goes. A part of me wants to laugh all night, go somewhere and hug everyone I've never been into. The other part of me wants to go to work, walk like a lady, talk slowly, and listen to all the stories I have never heard. We're all torn between who we are and who we want to be, what we do and what we wish we'd be doing, who we dream of loving and who we really love.

"We're all two people trapped in the body of one," the voice of me repeated. We all talk to ourselves, even if in reality we never let it out. We're all good and bad at the same time, good for some people and bad for others. We're all something we can never explain, we're all something no one will ever understand.

The party was almost over. The spotlights were being turned off one after the other. The music was getting calmer, and the songs slower. The place was less crowded. Everything was coming to an end. I didn't want to go back to reality. I started imagining my coming three hundred and sixty-five days. I imagined a piece of heaven.

"It's real, all that you can imagine is real," the voice of my Rose said.

"Because you can't imagine something you don't know, because you only imagine the things that you know of" I added. It made sense. If this is the life I dream of. It's surely the life I'll be living.

We were the last people in the place. The last song was played. Everything ended. The flower arrangement was taken away. I took some of the flowers then joined the rest of my friends again.

"What next?" Mateo asked.
"Home?" Jamila said.
"After-party for sure!" Naomi added.
"Nobody's home! We can go to my place."
"Are you sure, Rose?" they all asked in one voice.
"Yes!"

I was going to spend the rest of the night alone anyway. My ghosts will be with me. They will be my only companion in my solitude. My sister will come home tomorrow. She is spending the beginning of the year with her best friend. They will watch a movie and then sleep peacefully. My mother is attending to the passengers of her flight and my stepfather never comes home when she's not there. So until then, I will try to talk to every ghost that I know, I will try to find comfort in my loneliness.

I was wishing with every little tear inside of me that the after-party would take place at my house. I wanted the night to end as good as it started. I talked to my ghosts about my solitude. I told them that everyone leaves me. I cried with them too. I don't know why my ghosts never leave. It scares me because everyone else is always away.

We went to my house. It felt different with people there. Loneliness is the only thing destroying me. We ordered pizza and gathered up in my room. Half the group were sitting on my pink couch, the other half were sitting on the floor facing the others. I was on the bed, waiting impatiently for my food. We started playing cards, singing songs, talking loudly, then slowly. They made my night worthwhile.

Just after they all left at 6am someone knocked on my door.

"Good morning," Adam said as he handed me a rose.
"I haven't slept yet!"

"May I allow myself to come in?"

"To leave, you mean. It's six in the morning. I'm never a good idea at this time."

"Don't forget your pills."

"Go away! I'm good! I don't want to see your face again. What kind of therapist are you?"

It was the first time that I realize that I'd never been to a hospital before. I was trying hard to remember the pieces of me that I left behind. I gave up on cancer.

***

Rose came running to me after I left her house. She finally told me that her cancer is not real. I've been waiting forever to hear this. Every doctor that I worked with tried to tell her that her bones never really hurt her. Every doctor knows that every extra cell is only in her imagination, in the body that she has, in the picture she forms inside of her. She finally came to terms with herself. Her life will be a lot easier now. She might never say a full goodbye to everything that she had but will surely welcome her new life with open arms. I left because Dan arrived to her place. He thought she'd just woken up... She hadn't even slept.

THIRTY

Today I celebrate myself for being cancer-free. It's a long time. I can't remember when I last had a chemotherapy session, I can't remember cancer being inside of me recently. Today I celebrate myself. I celebrate the fact that I am where I have always wanted to be. I celebrate the only lesson that life has ever taught me. Life is what you make it, life is right here.

We crave the extra mile, we are addicted to effort. We always have in our minds the thought that everything we search for is hidden somewhere we're not, so we run to that place, and every place leads to another. The truth is, everything is where you decide to search for it. Happiness is not a mystery, happiness is inside of you, and you will find it. You will reach it when you understand that you don't need to run miles for it. Success isn't on the other side of the continent, it's not in the university you will never attend, it's not in the job you have never done, it's in you. It's all about what you do with the little things you are able to hold in your hands. The only real obstacles are the ones your own mind creates. In other words, you are your biggest obstacle, so you better deal with yourself otherwise.

Today, as I celebrated my wellness, I ran for a mile all alone in the neighborhood. I wasn't conscious at all, I was just running, trying to run inside my mind the series of memories I have had all my life. It was like a movie, a song that was always on replay, something that would never fade away, no matter how many times I tried to erase it. Engraved inside of me are the moments I have lived, and the people I have met, the places I have visited and the strangers I have smiled at. We change as we live. I could have been a totally different person, I could have had another soul, but the universe has put me in this mould, to be shaped this way and to then shape a detail of the lives of the people I meet.

When you live strongly and deeply for some time, you might find you are living with a fragmented heart. It's not the bad fragmented heart that we hear about in sad movies, it's not a feeling of emptiness, but the feeling of being everywhere at the same time, the feeling of having the world inside of you because you left pieces of you in every place you have been to and in the people that you loved.

The first time I ever traveled by train, I couldn't understand the pictures of the different landscapes that were running so quickly right under my eye. It was a changing story with every changing mile. I was watching, smiling and daydreaming about the lives happening in these frames. I couldn't say a word, until the train stopped and then I started reforming the pictures inside my mind. I started understanding why a piece of me was still there appreciating the beauty of the place and the other piece of me was inside my own mind, connecting to my sensations the joy my eyes captured.

The pieces of us are always connected to one another, so when we leave a part of who we are in a person, or in a place, it never goes away, and it's hard to pick the pieces you left back up and run away with them once again. I have understood why when we try to forget all that we have lived, every detail that has happened to us will remind us slowly and forcibly to relive it. Yes, it has always been real, everything around us reminds us of everything that has happened to us.

Nostalgia is a liar, it lets us hold on to the past, so we give up on having a better present. We let go before even trying and we bury ourselves in the same place where we have buried all of our memories.

THIRTY-ONE

The ghosts of us come and go, and they change how we behave with time. The ghosts of us either help us or haunt us, in the most authentic yet wicked ways ever. They haunt us when they hear us and we become monsters, only until we realize we are humans, lovers, helpers, and every other thing in disguise. I'm going somewhere, I'm going to tell Dan about it now.

"I'm leaving."

"Where are you going, Rose?"

"I don't know, I'm just going somewhere, and we're all going somewhere too."

"I can't understand you…"

"Sometimes you can't understand where you're going either, or where you want to go, but eventually you figure out halfway through, you just have to be on the road."

"What do you mean?"

"Dan, when your intuition tells you that you need to leave, don't stay."

"But you will need to come back to this place one day."

"I will leave, even if one day I get a need to be back here."

This conversation was in my room, I don't know what he understood, but his eyes were somehow looking at me strangely. I felt like I didn't like him as I used to before. I used to talk to him even when I was talking to myself. Now I barely mentioned his name. I kissed him, and told him that I had to leave.

I start walking to my car to go meet a stranger in a place that I still don't know. Yes, I will have a conversation with a stranger today. They will tell me the story of their life, and maybe I will do the same. Maybe on another day, in another life, or in this one, I will take a stranger for a deep talk in my car, or in my favorite bar. I will let them try my favorite cocktail or eat my favorite pizza if they crave the same way too. I will spend a day with a stranger, because today, I understood again that we are more alike than we will ever realize. I might be different, but my story isn't, and some of the details will relate to the details of your story.

As Dan left my house, I got in the car and drove all night to go somewhere I'd never been to, to meet someone I'd never talked to.

He called me many times, but I didn't answer, because I didn't want to change my mind. I sang a few songs on the highway and drove to Starbucks, parking my car in front of the door vertically. I didn't care about the police or any people. I just wanted some coffee to let me continue the night happily. As I was waiting for my coffee, I grabbed an empty paper bag that I found on the table behind me and started folding it in various origami shapes. I was folding the paper bag slowly, thinking about everything and anything the stranger I would be meeting in a few minutes would be telling me.

"Rose, Rose..."
"It's me, thank you," I smiled.

The old lady who handed me my coffee had one of those smiles that hit your heart directly. I wasn't sure if a smile could ever feel this warm. I smiled back. I left. I got into my car, and started driving again.

The highway was crowded, it was five in the morning, I'm not sure. I didn't want to meet any stranger, so I decided to go home, and sleep more. As I parked my little white car in front of my building I heard the sound of Dan's motorbike blocking the entrance yet then I saw his bike which was already parked. I didn't know how or why I had heard its sound.

"Where were you?"
"Who the hell are you? Why are you even here?"
"Where were you, Rose?"

"Starbucks."

"I came to spend the night."

"It's morning, can't you see?"

"I came to spend the morning, I'm sorry."

"I need to sleep."

I pushed him and went straight to my cozy room. I didn't even notice that he had come in right after me. I needed to sleep. I needed change. I didn't need anything that I already had, or anyone that I already knew. I went to bed without a single word. I slept in the middle of the bed. I usually sleep on one side. I didn't even bother keeping the door open. He came in and I moved to the side of the bed, to avoid the conflict that was about to take place. He slept next to me. It was the first time ever that we slept next to each other without me being in his arms. I usually hug him, until I fall asleep, and he usually makes sure that I'm deeply sleeping before letting go of me. This time, everything was different. We weren't mad at each other, we weren't bored — but a pause in time is always a relief. A pause in time to break the usual is always needed.

I woke up at four in the afternoon and he had gone. He'd woken up early, and left. I'm not sure if he was even here. It was alright, I was leaving too. I was fooling around with everyone, and no one would ever stop me.

I walked into an open buffet restaurant. I didn't find a table at first but I walked straight to the salad bar. I filled my plate with only two types of salad, a Greek salad and a coleslaw. It was perfectly split from the middle as if I had drawn a line. I was holding a Coke in the other hand.

As I was wandering around the chairs and tables of the restaurant, I kept making eye contact with anyone that I felt could be comforting or welcoming to me. At last, I found a sixty something year old lady eating alone. I allowed myself to sit at her table before speaking.

"I'm sorry, I don't want to eat alone, my name is Rose."
"Are you serious?"

Her "Are you serious?" sounded too firm. I thought she was going to leave this place because of me — even though she was smiling.

"My name is Rose, Rosaline, but everyone calls me Rose," she went on to say.
"I'm different. My real name is Rose. I am a rose. You will figure out what I mean later."
"Why are you here? Why are you alone?"
"I needed to surround myself with people who don't know me, people who won't understand me."
"People who don't know your story."
"Yes, Rosa, Rosal."
"Rosa, I like it, you can call me Rosa."

I smiled and she continued talking, all the time looking into my eyes. I think she was trying to see me on the inside. I saw passion; she was interested. No one was ever that interested while talking to me. Maybe because it was just the beginning, and beginnings are always exciting, or maybe because I was still a mystery to her, and humans love mysteries.

I want to hold her hand.
I'm scared.

"I work in the bookstore next door. I come to eat here almost everyday. Everyone knows me, but no one has ever initiated a conversation with me."
"I hate that."
"No, Rose. There's no need to hate that. It's the people you know yet don't know at the same time. The people you hear about, but never talk to. So you keep wondering if what you know about them is truly who they are."
"But neither of you ever said a word."
"Eyes speak my dear. You are still young, you will understand this later. You will understand that you don't need a conversation to get to know someone."
"And sometimes, many conversations are never enough to understand someone."

We talked non-stop, mentioning everything that could possibly be mentioned. I didn't eat anything after my salad, because I didn't want to interrupt the talk to move to the buffet. I was enjoying every word she was saying. This person couldn't be a stranger. I felt like she was twinned with my life. She reminded me of Ares when she said what he had also said: "I didn't waste my years, I have seen every detail in life, listen to me."

I listened to her, I listened to everything she said, it made sense, it made perfect sense. I decided to talk to strangers all the time, some of them knew me better than anyone who was known to me. Some people have something in their hearts that makes them so close to the world. They send their energies everywhere they go.

I hate the people who know me, and that I know, but that aren't my friends. I hate the people who once knew me, but don't know me anymore. It makes me sad. They know something, they look at you like you're an open book, and you look at them back like they're one of your friends but you never dared to say goodbye to them before leaving a place, never dared to smile at their face. Who are they? It's hard and weird to explain. I somehow wished Rosaline was younger, someone my age, so I could take her with me everywhere. On my way home, I started imagining her as a man. If her soul had been put in a man's body, I wondered what could have happened to me; I would surely fall in love deeply.

My biggest problem wasn't cancer, or sadness. My biggest problem was always wanting to fill the empty spaces the universe had created in my life. I was always searching for all that was unfindable, always craving the unreachable. I told myself that part of me always looked for love. A part of me speaks about love as if it was an accomplishment. But no, finding the 'love of my life' isn't what I was created for. He is going to come, he's already here, even if he might seem wrong — but he's not all that matters to me.

When I got home, I didn't feel the same about this place. It was empty and I started hating being alone. I wanted to run, I wanted to have another conversation with someone who would understand me well. I went on the roof for the first time. It was cold and the place was full of dust and dirt but I didn't want to sit alone where I have always been sitting. I found a nice corner up there and I sat down slowly facing the street. I was almost leaning on the fence with my legs. I started talking to myself; thinking about who I really was, where I was and where I was going.

All my life, I have always thought that we are all going somewhere. We are walking, running, and standing at the same time. We crave people, we love people, and the last thing that matters to us is what is wrong, and what is right. Life was never split into wrong and right, or good and bad. It's more than this. I think it's all about what hits us on the inside, what we get attached to, and what scares us, bores us, and shreds us into pieces. Everyone is kind in a way. At least, everyone is kind to the ones they care about. Not everyone is sweet, lovable and caring but everyone has something in them that will make them good no matter how many times they follow what's bad. Some people, sinners, might be better than all the ones who have never sinned. People who are honest with one another, people who are honest with themselves. People who are honest with what they desire and what they dislike. People who try and fail, who try again in a different way. People who live and relive, and change. People you respect no matter how many times they did everything wrong. The people we met, the people we will never meet. The strangers, the friends, the ones that aren't strangers, but aren't yet friends. The parties, the nights that end, the mornings that you spend well. The life you have dreamed of, the life you have opened your eyes to, the dream you haven't brought to reality yet, and the reality that has turned into a dream. Your biggest fear, the thing that makes you cry. Your guilty pleasure, your secret desire. Your first love, your last love, the first person you ever hate. The people in your life, your first mad kiss, that tear you'll never forget, that mistake you'll never be strong enough to forgive, the one who has broken your heart, but that you still secretly love. Your mother, your father, and the family that you miss although you live with. The long lost family member that you secretly appreciate more than your closest relatives. The teacher who changed your life. The place you love the most in your house, the place that makes you feel safe. The one word that changes your day. Your favorite restaurant, your favorite ice cream flavour. The conversation that hit you so hard. The loss that made you cry. The loss that was the beginning of everything else, and the end of the grief over any other loss. Your first success, you first tear of joy, your first lunch with your earned money...

I kept thinking about all of this, until I was almost falling asleep so I stood up slowly, walked downstairs to my fridge while shaking my head to see my curls move and grabbed a bottle of orange juice. I drank a few sips right away from the bottle, then took it with me to my room. I was too tired to change into my pajamas, but I was wearing skin tight jeans that I would never be able to sleep in. I left the bottle of orange juice next to me on my nightstand, and I threw myself on my bed. My hands were too tired to undress my body, so I just slipped my jeans slowly with my feet. I kept my sweatshirt on. I slept, uncovered and I didn't move all night long.

The next morning I woke up as fresh as anyone could ever be. I had to have breakfast with Dan but I didn't want to see him. Whilst he was with me I decided to write him a letter and give it to him as he was leaving and wait for his reaction. I sat on the floor, grabbed a pencil, an eraser, a very old piece of paper, and started writing as I was saying it out loud.

"Dan, I never missed anyone that much before. You changed. I don't know. The only thing I know is that I have never loved someone that much or respected someone that much, even when they were as disrespectful as you were. The problem with you and me is that the love we had left a long time ago. All that is left is the comfort, and the joy we bring to each other. At a certain point you understand that the most important thing about love, is what is left of it when it's all gone because the memory of love is stronger than love itself. We still have something, it's not the goodnight kisses and

190

horror stories we used to share, but the meals and memories that have never stopped being there. It's about time that our story ends, Dani, I'm sorry, but I keep comparing our days to the days when it all began. The beginning of our story was the beginning of a new life to me. You are this person who changed something about the person I am. The first hug that makes you melt and fall to the other person's arms, the first time someone holds your hand and it feels like they held all of you. The first fight that makes you go to bed crying, the first "I'm sorry" that makes you worry that it would be rejected. The first date, the first smile. The first time that I get drunk with someone, the first time that someone wakes me up one hour after I sleep. You were the reason I do so many things for the first time, and today, I think I will leave you, and cry over someone I still love, but lost. I love you. And I'll heal my own heart for the first time too."

"Are you sure you want to leave?"
"I want to leave, but I don't want you to leave."
"I can't wait for you to make up your mind forever, Rose."
"I'm sorry, I have to say goodbye!"

We cried. And I left in search of the same kind of love in someone else, at times when I never found it. I met a lot of people, but each time it only made me want to go back to him more than the time before it. I will see him again, because I have a feeling that the universe has left something that will reunite us. I trust my intuition, I trust the universe, and I trust Dan, no matter how many times he tried to break my trust.

It's been years. It's been relationships, memories, and everything else that could come in between. I'm not ready for the same story to happen again. It's like someone asking me to start my cancer all over again. I'm not the person who would swallow their pride twice for the same person. I already swallowed my pride, walked over everything that I had and everything that I was for him. It's not that he's bad, it's not that he's good. It's going to take time. But you will understand that some people are only bad to you. You will understand that good people can be bad to you, and bad people good to you. You will understand that the way you define a person never truly reflects the way they are. People never show all their sides to everyone. Sometimes it's better if you barely know a person. A commonplace conversation might be better than a deep one. Sometimes empty words will tell you much more than any detail you will ever hear. It's going to take time, but sometimes you will have to walk away, even when every piece of you wants to stay. Sometimes, you will be forced to stay, but if your intuition tells you that something's wrong with the person standing in front of you, run away.

You don't have to explain yourself. Whatever life has done to you, whatever you have done to life, does not prove to anyone who you are. You just need to have things clear in front of your own eyes.

THIRTY-TWO

I'm going home, and I'll never say goodbye once more. I'm going back to where I belong, to find again who I once was. I'm never letting go of my true self, never trading my conscious side for anything else. I'm going home, home is the only place where I'll be able to find myself and face the torments that my mind tries to set.

"Who are you?" I asked a stranger. He ran away. I kept wondering what could have possibly been scary about me until I realized that he left because he saw bits of the psychopath he is through the psychopath that just asked him about himself.

Our eyes reveal a lot, and so does the way we smile. I remembered Ares at that moment. A stranger I will never forget, because I definitely found a friend in him.

I'm going home. There are no strangers at home but the ghosts who live with me are always near. There's a room at the end of my house that I never enter. It's full of people that I know nothing about, but that I tend to see a lot. There's a bathroom next to my room that has ghosts in its mirror. I'm sure, because every time that I look through it I see something I knew nothing about before. After I go home, I will make sure to walk in every corner of the apartment. I will make sure not to respond to any of the ghosts who keep wandering around. They will call my name, they will try to listen to my soul, they will fail to hear my voice.

"But Rose, you can't miss people that you have never known."

"Oh my God! Another ghost!"

"Calm down. Calm down, Rose. Go to your room, have a slice of chocolate cake, then analyze the situation."

I went to my room and sat on my pink couch, quiet yet shaking with fear. I started closing my eyelids very slowly and gently. I kept repeating the word silence in my mind until the only thing I was able to hear was the sound of my inner "shh".

I opened my eyes again and started crying until I remembered what the Rose inside of me had said, "Self control… Silence… Self control."

I started calming myself down. It took time, because every time I would feel better, a tear would drop again, and with every teardrop that would fall off my eye, I would start screaming again. I would start screaming, shouting, and talking to people I know nothing about. Some of them were once in my life, but most of them haven't yet lived. It took me a very long time to compose myself but I was only getting better. I think I was getting better. A ghost asked, "Rose, how could you miss people that you've never known?" It sounded like the voice of a very old man. He only had an upper body but he was able to fly. He couldn't walk. He glided around as he whispered words into the ears of fragile people like me (unlike me in a few minutes, hours, days, weeks, months, years…) .

I took off my socks, grabbed the cushion that was on the side of the couch and hugged it. I was shaking, terrified of losing my war with the ghosts. I started talking to myself slowly as if I were talking to a friend. "Rose. Your name is Rose. Your name is real, so real in the way it reflects everything you are or will ever be. Your parents named you Rose to reflect the beauty of a flower and the power of its fragrance. Rose, you are everything a rose is or will ever be. You are beautiful, but you are fragile. It's fine, as long as you take care of who you are, and what you need. Rose, you are everything we are able to feel, and everything that makes this world happy to be a part of the universe."

I stood up all of a sudden. I started walking around the house touching objects. I began drinking a few sips from the many bottles of wine that I had kept for so long in my room. I had fifteen glasses, placed in a row, and each filled with a different amount of wine. After my fifteenth sip, I took my glass of rosé wine and continued my walk in the apartment. I started talking to myself again as I was arranging some roses that I found in the living room. I found twenty-three white roses.

I'm twenty-three years old today. Roses remind me of someone, of something. Having fifteen glasses of wine tells me something too. Everything has a meaning in my world.

I slowly counted, arranged, and rearranged the twenty-three white roses in the most artistic ways. Artists will change the world. They express themselves. They don't add anything to the world, they don't invent anything, but unlike most of us, they are able to pull from the universe the right colors, fragments, drawings, photographs, and words.

I took one rose in a hand, and my glass of rosé in the other. I went back to my couch. I left my wine on the floor, and as I rested my body completely, I started talking to the rose I was holding. I started whispering words, and telling stories. I started dealing with this rose as if it was a clone of me. A mirror in which my soul was revealed.

"Loneliness," the rose in my hand said to the Rose inside of me. The rose in my hand told the Rose inside of me that loneliness can make things happen. The bad kind of things. Like talking to someone you don't know, or whispering words to ears that you don't even see. It's like seeing a black rose in front of you. It's like missing someone who's never been in your life in the first place, or telling someone a story you've never lived. Emptiness is not what you get after a loss. It's not the place that stays in your heart long after the moment or the person is gone, but the urge to create something, the urge to fill in every space inside of you. It's when you want to be everyone, and have everything at the same time. It's when you're too full to be empty, yet feel too empty to be full.

May all your memories keep you going. May the little world you live in tell you everything about the universe that has once created you. May you be powerful enough to know how powerless you are. May you be powerful enough to believe in the other powers of the universe.

THIRTY-THREE

I feel relieved. The war inside of me is fading away. The world is truly mine. The world belongs to me before I belong to the world. Everything that I want from the world is inside of me. I can see myself as I improve. I can watch my own progress. My satisfaction is constantly pushing me to want to be better and do more.

I understood that I have to take the lead, because if I don't control my own life someone else will do it for me. I have to have my own plans, my own dreams and my very own destiny. I have to make my own choices before the universe makes them for me. I have to start getting things done. I will start accomplishing tasks. I will do myself a little checklist every week or two. I will write myself notes. I will hang them on my wall.

"Note number one," I spoke to my own mind. "You're good, Rose. You don't have cancer. Note number two: You are everything that you decide to be. Note number three: I'll leave it blank for now… I'll write it later!"

There's hope. There's something inside of me that wants me to be at my best, even when I'm at my worst.

My phone screen lit up with a message. It was Louis and Jamila on our group chat.

Louis: Lunch at my place today… Who can make it?
Jamila: I still have work! I might catch you guys tonight. Have fun.
I watched my screen for a while, then I decided to answer them. As I was typing Naomi and Mateo were typing too. I waited to see what they were about to send.
Naomi: I'll come at night. We could watch a movie. I can't leave the office anytime soon.
Mateo: I'm out of town! I'll see you guys when I'm back! I have chemotherapy…Wish me luck.
I had to reply at that time: We love you Mateo, you'll be better than ever. Kisses!
Naomi: Where are you today, Rose?
"I'm on my way… I'm coming, Louis! Wait for me!" I said loudly as I was typing the words into my phone, ending them with a smiling emoji.

Louis called me right away, I answered faster than I ever did before.

"Where are you?"
"Driving."
"To where?"
"Never mind, I'll go back home," I said while laughing.
"No, no, no! I'm sorry... I'm waiting for you!"
"Bye!"

This was by far the most exciting phone call I had ever received. I couldn't wait to have lunch with Louis, I was so happy that no one could make it but me. I needed to talk to him about a lot of things.

I arrived to my destination, turned the music off, and took all the time I needed to park my car correctly. I got out and took the stairs to his apartment. I counted every step that I took on the stairway of his building. Thirty-three steps! By some kind of magic, I was able to take the stairs and my bones didn't feel like they were breaking into a million little pieces. Everything was an illusion. I was finally waking up!

His bell wasn't working. This guy was already getting on my nerves. I was always the one who used to get on his nerves, things were changing. I rubbed my hands together, took a deep breath, raised my right eyebrow and started making some noise at his door. He had to run before it broke.

I went in and ran straight to the kitchen to see what he had prepared.

"Surprised I came?"
"No!"
"I had to come and cook with you!"
He laughed and so did I.
"So, what do you want to eat?"
"A salad?"
"And steak! With..."
"Pasta?"
"No, french fries!"

I went to wash my hands, then came back to the kitchen.

***

When Rose came back to the kitchen I was cutting the potatoes. I stopped the knife for a moment and stared at her. This kind of friendship is very rare. We've known each other for a very long time. I don't think that other people have this kind of comfort. She supports me, I support her. She acts like a parent sometimes. The two of us will never fall in love with each other, we're too unveiled in front of each other.

"I don't know how to deal with this thing," she said as she pulled the raw steak from the fridge.
"Leave it, you can start with the salad," I told her as I gave her a knife.

"Where are the others?"

"They have a life to live," she replied.

"Impressive!"

"Can I tell you something?"

"No! Because it will just be that you can't even make a salad."

"Yes, but I will prove you wrong. Can you get me cheese from behind you?"

"I don't like cheese in salads."

"I don't care! You will like my salad!"

***

My salad bowl looked like a work of art. It's something I had never done before. I felt so happy with it. The smallest things make me smile now. Everything makes a difference, after all. We should see the greatness of little things. My steak was ready and Louis had prepared the fries.

"Lunch is served!" we both said at the same time. We looked at each other's faces and laughed until we almost cried. It was hilarious. I rubbed my hands together, held a bottle of lemonade and a bucket of ice, and followed him as he was holding our plates.

We went on the balcony. He knew how much I preferred outdoors over indoors. I like it when things are limitless. I like nature. I like the wind, the sun, the moon, and the sky that holds the world together. I believe in the universe, its powers and its signs. He had a vase of white roses on a side table. It was beautiful. His place is tiny but cozy.

"Seeing you being better is making me happy, Rose."

I smiled for a while then said, "The world has changed me, so I decided to change the world."

"Go on..."

"I was afraid at first. Everything is hard until you start. The first step is always the hardest. Everything that follows comes with ease. Life is a war. You have to destroy everything before it destroys you. Life will eventually kill you, because death is part of life and stronger than will. You don't have to accept everything, but you will have to let everything happen to you."

Someone knocked at the door and interrupted my conversation with Louis. I went to see who it was.

"Hey, Rose."

"Naomi! Tell me how you've been?"

"It's nice to see you here."

"It's not like you didn't know I'd be here."

"Where is Louis?"

I didn't even bother telling her where he was. I kept walking and she followed me to the balcony. It was almost 7pm. I had to go back home. I didn't have to, but I wanted to.

"Bye, guys! Thanks for today, Lou!"

"Bye, Rose, take care."

I drove home and slowly started crying. It became hysteric after a while. I was thinking of how I wanted my life to be. I could imagine something, I had it all planned in my head. I decided to call Adam. I wanted to see him.

"Hey, it's Rose."
"I know your number by heart now!"
"Can I see you today?"
"Where are you?"
"Going home."
"Do you want to go for coffee or something?"
"Can you come over? It would be a lot easier for me."
"Okay, I'm on my way."

I had to arrive before Adam. I wanted to shower and change into something comfortable. I wanted to be at my best. I wanted to talk freely about everything that annoys me without dropping a tear from my eye.

I arrived, and by the time I had reached my room, the doorbell rang.

"I got home fast!"
"Just for me?"
"You want coffee?"
"No, tea."
"And cake?"
"Who baked it?"
"Me! I told you everything has changed!"

"I'll taste it and tell you if you're a good chef."

"I've always been good at everything."

"Overly confident, Rose."

"How are you Adam?"

"Not better than you!"

"I'm serious. How's everything going in your life?"

"I don't know."

"Why are you even a therapist?"

"I never asked myself that question. I just happen to be one… Did you see Dan?"

"I might call him tonight."

"It's already night."

"I mean before I sleep."

"Are you sure?"

"Don't start this conversation it bothers me a lot."

The conversation didn't bother me, it was the memories. I wanted to move forward with my life. He was everything in my past, I didn't want it all to come to me again. I was still in love with him. It's very hard to let go at first. When you love someone with all your heart, time doesn't heal your broken heart but breaks it more. Dan had dug very deep into my soul but I needed someone new. I needed to feel the excitement that comes with every beginning.

"Do you want to watch a movie?"

"What movie do you want us to watch?"

"I don't know, Adam!"

"Charlie Chaplin?"

"If you want to."

We started watching the movie, eating popcorn and drinking soda. We were too tired to talk, the words didn't want to come out of our mouths. A problem was starting to appear: Adam was not just a therapist to me. He was a friend. He was getting closer to me. If I didn't have Dan in the background, I would have surely fallen in love with Adam. I see him more than I see my friends. We were doing everything together. We sometimes met at the grocery store, took a walk to the nearest restaurant, had breakfast together. We spent hours and hours together and our silences were now comforting and not awkward. He left right after the movie ended because I was already half asleep. I was very tired, the kind of tired that makes you relieved when you're in bed.

Today was good, tomorrow will be better.

THIRTY-FOUR

I was right when I told myself that tomorrow would be better. I woke up feeling that everything that had happened to me was an illusion, an abstraction that was somehow never there in the first place. I was having breakfast with Jamila today. I showered, got dressed, had some juice, prepared myself as if I was going to an office job, and rushed to my car.

"Are you up?"
"Yes, I'm waiting for you."
"I'll be there in two minutes!"

It was the shortest phone call I've ever made. I like when things are short, they make more sense, they have more meaning. I might allow myself to compare my mornings now to my mornings a few weeks ago. I used to go to bed crying, and wake up struggling to open my eyes again, because of the pain my tears had caused me. I was mad at the world, so the world was mad at me. Now I had decided to make peace with myself. I had to make peace with the world too. Every time something good happens, every time I become stronger, every time I find a reason to be better.

"Life has reasons," I told myself.
"Rose, you have always repeated those three words," the ghost of me said.

It doesn't bother me. I will repeat them every time my ears need to hear them. I will repeat them every time my soul needs them. I will repeat them every time my heart tries to listen to the sound of them. They have to keep resonating inside of me.

"Rose, life has reasons," I repeated.
"Rose, life has reasons," the ghost of me repeated in my voice.

***

Rose is having breakfast with Jamila today. I'm trying to keep an eye on her most of the time. Adam asks me about her a lot. We're all standing by her side because we see something in her. She deserves to live without the dreams that haunt her, and the realities that only happen inside of her. I've always been one of her closest friends, but I've never fully understood all that happens to her. I never truly listened to her when we were younger. When she would start talking about the things that came to her in her sleep, and that sometimes used to come with her everywhere she went I used to laugh. I would tell her that these jokes were way too old.

"Louis! I'm serious!" She would scream to my face until I would hug her tightly begging her to forgive me. Rose has her reasons, it all started when we first knew that Mateo was hit by cancer. Her story started as his chemotherapy began. When I think alone, when I think of Rose's life slowly, I find myself capable of analyzing why she unconsciously dissociates herself from reality. But it's very confusing and I don't know how to deal with her case anymore. She needs to see a psychiatrist because everything we tell her will never be enough to heal her.

***

I arrived. I was very cold and anxious. I didn't want people to see me. When I'm like that it scares me, it makes me feel like I'm not who I really am. Jamila has always shown me a lot of love. I know I mean a lot to her. All my friends tend to love me more than they love each other. I never understood the reason, I never found myself that lovable. I never saw myself the way they see me. I can't picture myself with all the beauty they picture me with. Maybe they have pity for me. I don't know. It scares me. If I ever find out that the love they have for me is not as real as it seems, a part of me will never come back to them. I waited in my car for a long time. Jamila finally showed up.

"Why are you so late?"

"I'm not… You just called me."

"Why do you always have an argument?"

My heartbeats are always faster than they're supposed to be. Sometimes I think that it's because I'm always very excited for everything, sometimes it's because of the excitement that never exists.

Jamila took me to a cozy bar near her place. It was easy to fall in love with it. It's one of those places that makes you want to think more, talk more, and open up to whoever you are with at any time of the day, and any time of the year. It killed the anxiety inside of me. The place was able to affect my soul. I started thinking about how every little detail that we encounter as we live is as powerful as anything that has once made us. The key to everything is to be comfortable. You are only capable of loving when you are comfortable. Here's to the places you fall in love with, here's to the memories you can't help but reminisce over. Here's to the thoughts, the words, the smiles, and the ideas that you can never let out of your heart.

"I want to do everything I have never done before."

"Rose?"

"I want to start thinking differently. I want to see my life improving. I need to understand exactly what is happening to me, and to my body. I can't live this way, pretending that I'm someone new everyday."

I was talking about stability. That's what I needed in my life. I didn't mean the kind of stability that would make you a very determined person, or that stability that will grant you the capability of determining every step that you take and every direction you walk in, but the stability that happens within the soul. I needed to feel calmer, healthier, happier. I needed to control my emotions, to stop bursting into tears without a very emotional reason. It's not what I once called self-control, I don't know what to call this. I understood what I wanted but the words the universe offers us are very limited compared to the amount of emotions that we feel. I was talking about that stability that makes you have a serene soul.

Sometimes my days would get better when I would force a smile on my face, because it became real with time. I could forget about a lot of my worries but they always came back. I needed to go slowly, and heal one part of me at a time, until I felt completely relieved. Jamila didn't respond to what I was saying. She was listening to me peacefully. We had a moment of silence, one of those moments that are capable of erasing the wars inside of you.

"I need to see a new therapist."

"What about Adam?"

"He's my friend now. He understands me. I talk to him about everything. But everything between us makes me want to hug him and fall into his arms."

"You like him?"

"I don't know. No, I guess, I don't know, maybe. I'm not sure."

The way I was expressing myself wasn't even close to being convincing. I knew she had to force herself to think that my heart still belonged to Dan. She wasn't wrong. Dan had my heart, but he never had my body. Adam attracted me. I'm easily able to picture his body with mine in my mind. I know that something's wrong with this. It's not related to anything that I had in the past, but to everything I want to have in the future. I feel excluded in this society. I feel unwanted everywhere that I go. It's tormenting. I don't know where life is taking me anymore. I have a surprise every morning and when I go to bed at night I get anxiety attacks and cry so much that it becomes impossible to sleep. The way I express myself does not reflect the way that I think. I'm very different on the inside. I need someone who would always want to know the real me more.

I left Jamila at four in the afternoon. We had spent nearly six hours together. This could possibly be the longest breakfast conversation she had ever had. I had to drive back home, I have a long way of thinking to go through. I drove to Jamila's house first to drop her off. I went in, stood up in front of a mirror to make sure that my curls were as curly as they're supposed to be, then I walked straight to her room. I wasn't able to talk. I didn't have anything to say. It was harder for me to express myself than it had ever been before. I started walking in circles in her room. I don't know where I was taking myself. I was waiting for her to come out of the shower to tell her that I was leaving. I knocked on her bathroom door.

"I'm leaving."
"No, wait, I got us some snacks… Stay for another hour."
"Be fast!" I screamed from behind her door.
"Don't worry Rose," she said with her loudest voice.

She finally came out wrapped in a white towel with her name embroidered on it. I stared at her. There was something about her wet, fresh skin. Something about the way she looked at herself in the mirror and the way she looked at me.

"Mateo's one lucky guy," I secretly told myself.

She grabbed her black sweatshirt and jeans and ran back to the bathroom. A part of me wished that she was going to change in my presence.

"Rose, what are you doing?" I told myself after I slapped my own face.

It's stronger than me, I know. I don't have an explanation to what I am doing. I need to wake up. I will force myself to walk on the right path again.

The bathroom is empty.

What am I doing?

Where am I?

Who is Jamila?

And who am I?

I spent the whole day with Jamila, the ghost of me told me, but I didn't know that at the time. I drove all night to reach my house. I drove all night because I took myself to streets I knew nothing about before. I kept imagining new roads. I was good until I arrived to my bed. I wanted to sleep but I couldn't close my eyes. I cried. I felt like there was something in my throat. I had a huge headache. I hate my constant anxiety. It's the same scene that keeps repeating itself over and over again.

I will try to breathe into the moment. I will hug my pillow, until I get better. I will hold my own hands, and control my own mind.

THIRTY-FIVE

"Good morning, Adam."

"Rose, how are you?"

"I need you to come."

"I'm on my way."

"As fast as you can, please."

I found him at my door five minutes after the end of our phone call. I wasn't feeling well at all. I needed someone to save me from myself. I needed someone who would save me from my thoughts. I could hear the sound of his footsteps as he walked slowly in. He hugged me in a way he had never done before.

I lay on the couch as he talked gently wiping away my tears as they fell but nothing would change the way I was feeling. I tried to compose myself but all my efforts were in vain. He took a deep breath and put his hand on my shoulder then held my hand. Everything suddenly changed and I began laughing, I don't know what kind of laughter it was. I started talking peacefully.

"I will never forget the day the doctor came to my room, held my hand, kissed my forehead and told me that I was well. My cancer was healed. I will never forget the tears he cried while hugging me. I was his success. He saved my life. It was something he felt grateful for. I remember every word he said, the sound of the monitors being turned off. "When you are as old as I am, there is nothing you can do but remember," Ares' voice said to me.

You will never understand until you reach my age. I have seen death so many times and every time it would approach me, it would turn away and go back to where it came from. I didn't die of cancer. Everyone thought I would. Apparently if I leave the world any time soon, it's only to leave a place for the newborns to live. I have been here for so long, I have been here long before I knew that my life will be drawn in the most beautiful colors of the palette. I don't know what to say. If life was huggable, I would have, without a doubt, kept it loved and warm in my arms forever. I learned that no matter what you have, no matter how big or small it is, find a place for it in your life, let it fit somewhere, because it matters.

So many things break my heart. The love I have for life is so much stronger than the love I had for any boy when I was a fool. It's vaster than anything words are capable of explaining. Life was good to me, because I was always good to it, and always kind to myself. Love life and it will love you back.

Until we meet again,

Rose."

I signed my words out loud, as if it were a letter I was speaking to Adam.

"Rose, come back to the this world. What are you telling me?"
"Why is it so hard for you to listen to me?"
"I've been listening to you for a whole lifetime, but you are locked inside your imagination, locked inside the world you have created for yourself. You have been believing in your thoughts so much that you stopped believing in the world, you aren't conscious of the reality you are living in."

I started to feel that something was wrong with me, and in me. Everyone was trying to convince me that my cancer was not real, that something was wrong with the stories that I was telling. I was confused. Were they trying to make me forget the pangs of pain I have always felt or was I living an unconscious life? Why were most people believing that unreal life of mine? How did I make it seem so real?

I think it's going to be complicated. I don't feel like I'm that mentally unstable. I appear very normal to almost everyone. Why are they trying to take me somewhere else? Why do they want me to go back to living with them?

"I don't want to go live with you, I want to keep my own house, everything in this place is more special than it is anywhere else."

"Rose, you live with us, you are with us."

I recall when my mother started crying. It was so strong she fell on the floor. She was falling apart from every side, her body was all over the place, and so were her tears. Everything about her daughter seemed unreal to her, but what was so wrong about me?

I am very conscious, so conscious that sometimes I can remember things that haven't happened to me, and I start reminiscing and then missing them. I tend to remember the days I spent at the hospital, my operations and my heart monitor. I know the nurses. And yet everyone keeps telling me that I have never entered an operation room. My mother tried to explain to me slowly but I burst into tears, pulled her hair and pushed her on the floor. My stepfather came to me. He started hugging me. He told me that I'm doing fine. I ran away from him and I started searching for my hair growth pills. I couldn't find them so I went to my sister and asked her if she knew, she told me that my hair looked perfectly fine. I started screaming and shouting. I didn't know where to go. My body was almost vibrating, my hands were shaking and my face turned red. My mother was on the floor trying hard to understand what was happening to me. My stepfather was running all over the house trying to find a way to get me out of this. My sister locked herself in her room. I stopped screaming and crying all of a sudden and I walked to the bathroom, locked the door, and sat on the floor, in the corner right behind the door. I started talking slowly to myself. I started understanding what was happening to me. I needed to stab myself somewhere, to understand that this life is real. What was so wrong about me? I am only twenty three years old. No, I am not old. No, I have never had cancer, I have never been waiting for my boyfriend to come to see me in my hospital room.

What happened inside of me? What happened to my dreams, to the life I wished for, to the success I craved? What happened to all the happiness I used to bring to my life and to the life of everyone that I loved? Why did I cut off my hair? Yes, I cut my hair. I'd lost some hair because I was stressed and I then I started relieving myself by cutting at it, then I thought that I had cancer and that chemotherapy had done all of that to me. I imagined going to places with my father alone. I imagined that years and years ago when he was here he took me to London for some kind of therapy. My father died a long time ago. I cried once over my grandmother, and I imagined the moment of her death, I kept convincing myself that nothing was ever hard to me as this goodbye, but then now, I must say, I never saw my grandmother in the first place.

This was all so wicked. What happened inside of me was truly wicked. How did I ever leave this world, how did I imagine another world? I gave myself another age, lived in another place, and told myself six million words that were insane.

Today I am going to see a therapist for real. I will tell them that I have struggled more than anyone their eyes have seen. Today I'm here, trying to draw my life for real. I have promised the world that I will take care of myself. I have promised myself too.

"Why did I let myself go to places like this with my mind?" I asked myself. "Why did I make it hard for me?"
I remained silent for a few minutes then I had to answer my own questions.
"Maybe, if I accepted the life the universe has given me, I would have lived more peacefully."
I think I'm starting to wake up. I'm starting to take the right step!

I know that ever since I was little, I was always trying to fill in the empty spaces I found in my life, then found in my heart, and in my mind. I know that ever since I started to understand life, I have seen people struggle. My friend almost died of cancer and I let myself imagine that it had happened to me.

I am leaving now, I will stop talking to myself, or maybe I will force myself to speak the right words, walk on the right path and think the right way. I will force myself to say words that will always keep me in this world. I will live a very simple life, I will be a very simple girl, with a very simple heart, and a very simple mind. I will stay away from every sadness, and every sorrow.

I will leave now. No, my body isn't hurting me like I used to say, no I'm not walking aimlessly in my hospital room, and no my life isn't as hard as I thought it was. I'm going to start from scratch, I'm going to control my mind. I will force myself to be conscious all the time. I might allow a space for my dreams to expand inside of me while I'm asleep, but I will never live a life that only exists in my dreams.

I will leave now. I am going to see a therapist and tell them that the universe has finally woken me up. The universe is capable of healing who we are. I hate pills. All kinds of pills. I don't want to start telling my story to this human being. I don't enjoy sharing who I am with the world. But I have to, I think, I'm not sure. I'm never sure.

I left now, and I am walking alone in an empty street. I am singing my thoughts out loud, hoping that this time, I start well enough to have peace inside of me for a lifetime.
I left a few minutes ago. I am coming back home when I am done. I have so much left for me to live the way that I want.

I left half an hour ago. I am still looking for the doctor's clinic. I know that I'll be lost for a while, I will forget about the reality I live in, and I will start dreaming of a life that isn't mine. It won't last long, I promised myself. Because as soon as I reach the clinic, I will lie on my therapist's bed and start telling them that sometimes I get out of my head.

I left thirty-four minutes ago and I'm only one minute away. I am going to hug my psychiatrist. I don't want to wait for my turn, but Sunday mornings are usually not that crowded.

I left thirty-five minutes ago, and I am only one step away from bringing myself back to life. The psychiatrist will ask me so many questions and will try to let me find an answer, but I already know what and how to reveal what's inside of me. I think that the psychiatrist will try to understand how after so many years of living away from this world, I started being conscious of the unconsciousness I've been having for so long.

It was quite a long session and he asked me to record the words that I let out of my mouth as I explained my life. He asked me to remember a lot of things, to try to distinguish the life the universe has granted me from the life my dreams have created. I was somehow relieved.

My session came to an end. I stood up somewhat erratically, took my little pink messenger bag, smiled naïvely, thanked Leonardo for listening to me for that long, and walked slowly out of the door. I started thinking at that time how much everything that happens inside of us matters more than everything that we truly live. Our bodies, after all, aren't as important or as meaningful as our souls. For a while, my soul was fragile, and so was my body, my thoughts, and everything that I ever was. Starting today, I feel like everything is falling into place. I'm not going to forget about the sadness or the psychological trouble that I had, because every time I remember, it will give me a will not to go back to that. It will remind me of the importance of having the Rose that I am beneath all that happens to me. I will measure how I was to where I am now. I will smile.

I am going down the stairs now, my legs aren't hurting me like I have always said. I don't feel as if my hair got any shorter than it was before.

I've started my thirty-five minutes walk back home. I turn my stopwatch on and I won't care if I reach home a bit later than I should. I will never be tough on myself again, I will let myself live, I will set myself free. I will accept whatever happens to me, with a smile on my face and faith in my heart. I believe, or I have started believing that the universe works for our well-being. We don't have to do anything more than what the universe makes us do, because our power is so little after all.

I am twenty-five minutes away from home and when I get home, I will take out a piece of paper and draw something. I will then spend some time alone to think slowly about my life. I will draw myself a path to walk on, and I will try to understand why my mother forgave me after all the pain I caused her, without receiving an apology. I will do so many things, because today, my life starts again. I am going to places I've never been to before, but this time I am taking my body with me, not just my mind. Our souls are made of everything yet nothing at all, so you never know how it goes.

I am fifteen minutes away from home, I am fifteen minutes away from going where I have always belonged.

I am only five minutes away from home, I don't feel any kind of pain in my body or even inside my brain.

Maybe whatever happened to me was because I once lost someone I never thought I would lose, maybe because someone who was perfectly fine, got hit by an illness. Maybe whatever happened to me happened because I somehow never grieved enough, I never let things fully happen to me in reality.

The worst thing anyone could ever do to themselves is to live half a life, fearing that the other half wouldn't make them as happy or satisfied. We are our own enemies, we are the weapon that works the most on our own destruction, and as soon as we start understanding this, as soon as we start accepting this, we give ourselves the chance and opportunity to move forward with our lives, and protect ourselves from who we are.

I understood that I was the one creating all of that. I decided that when I got home I would run straight to the kitchen, to eat everything that I thought I couldn't easily eat. I would then run to my mother, hug her more than I ever had and cry slowly in her arms. I would cry of happiness, of satisfaction, and of thankfulness. I would tell the world that the Rose inside of me will never die, no matter how many times I have slowly tried to kill it. I would tell the world that the Rose inside of me does not shut down, no matter how much you stop watering it. I would tell the universe that my name is

Rose, that my name is real, so real for the way it reflects everything I am or will ever be. I would tell the universe that I was stuck somewhere for so long, that I found my way out, and that now, the Rose inside of me knows better than it has ever known, about the stories I have never lived and the words that I have never heard. The Rose inside of me lives every moment life has given her, the Rose inside of me understands people and feels their souls. The Rose inside of me might sometimes be fragile, but so is the universe. The Rose inside of me feels so deeply, everything that her eyes can see. The Rose inside of me will never say goodbye to such a happy yet sad world.

THIRTY-SIX

The music is loud and the different beats are all over the place, striking the different parts of the Rose inside of me.

We all listen to the same music in a different way. We all hear the same beat differently. The music is loud and I'm part of the noise. I'm as cheerful as anyone could ever be. The lights are moving over me. The excitement has never been that real. I wonder if every year will be as good. I wonder if I will always be as happy.

"Everything is between our hands, everything is within who we are," the Rose inside of me tells me. Her voice strikes me louder than the sound of the music. We will be good, we will never stop improving, as long as we're walking on the right path or admitting that we're on the wrong one.

I promised myself that the end of this night will be the beginning of my new life.

The music is loud and so is my soul tonight. I'm dancing with everyone in the place. Everyone is as happy. We're all standing in the same place. The energy is also very loud. The kind of loud that strikes everything and everyone no matter who they are, where they are or who they are with.

It's almost midnight. The countdown is five minutes away. I don't know how this year will be. I'm very excited. Or at least I think I am.

"Come on! Why are you so late?"
"What is it, Louis?"

Louis takes me by the hand and pushes me until we reach the microphone like we did last year. The music is getting louder and louder, and the people are dancing more. Each of us is in their own corner, while we are all waiting for the same thing and standing in the same place.

"Ten!" I scream.
All the voices follow mine.
"Nine! Eight! Seven! Six!"
"Five!" I say so close to the microphone that my lipstick leaves a stain on it.
"Four! Three! Two!"
"One!"

"Happy New Year!"

The whole place screams in one voice and yet I can recognize every voice within it. The energy speaks louder than anything else in this place. We have finally reached our destination. It is surely a very happy new year.

Contact the author:
aminachalach@hotmail.com
instagram and twitter: @aminashalash

SUMMARY

Imprimé sur papier **Clairefontaine** fabriqué dans les Vosges.

Achevé d'imprimer sur les presses de l'imprimerie
Centre Littéraire d'Impression Provençal
www.imprimerieclip.fr
contact@imprimerieclip.fr